# Alpha Beta Gamma

# Alpha Beta Gamma

*The Sloppy Sleuth and Trio Spy Thriller Series*

Malabika Ray

# Alpha Beta Gamma

Woven against the backdrop of the contemporary world affairs around us, all characters and events in this story are fictional.

Second Edition: Published on April 2025
Author: Malabika Ray
(malabika.ray.author@gmail.com)

Proof Editing: Keiran Devaney

Cover Design: Nick Castle

Copyright © 2024 Malabika Ray
All rights reserved.

**ISBN:** 9789153114291

Malabika Ray

# Dedication

To all the sloppy and nerdy sleuths around the world …

## *Prologue*

Tehran, October, 2022

It is past seven o'clock in the evening. Sitting on the living room sofa, Nasser Ali is reading the newspaper, and his wife, Fatemeh, is making the dinner in the kitchen. They are both waiting for their daughter Sara to return. They always have dinner together.

Through the window of her kitchen, Fatemeh can see the sky transitioning from a brilliant orange to a deep purple, casting a warm glow over the landscape. The Alborz Mountains in the distance are silhouetted against the fading light, their rugged peaks providing a beautiful backdrop.

Usually, Sara comes back from University before six. She has just joined Tehran University to do her Masters in Psychology. But this morning, before leaving for the Uni, she told her mother that she might be a little late. Even though she did not say, Fatemeh knows why. Sara is taking part in the protests.

# Malabika Ray

This is one of those protests that started a few weeks back and since then has spread like wildfire through the length and breadth of the country. This is the protest against the brutality of the morality police. This morality police have always been unpopular among liberal, educated segment of the society. Fatemeh remembers how she and her friends used to hate them when she was in college, almost thirty years back.

But this undercurrent of hatred has reached a whole new level after the death of Masha Amini, a twenty-two-year-old university student who was savagely beaten by the morality police. The government had wanted to tackle the protests heavy-handedly from the outset, as they always do. But this time it did not work well. People have literally taken to the streets. As expected, young people, especially university students, are at the forefront of this movement. But they also got a lot of support from their parents.

Even though the state-controlled media tried to suppress the news and even cracked down on social media, they have not been fully successful. #MashaAmini is trending heavily on social media and international support is pouring in. After doubling down on their acts initially, the government has also softened their stance as various officials, including the provincial government, has expressed their regrets for Masha's death.

# Alpha Beta Gamma

Yet the protesters are regularly being beaten, detained, and harassed in all possible ways, by the authorities. That is why Fatemeh started feeling a bit anxious. Sara was supposed to return by seven, now it is almost eight. Even though she supports her brave daughter, as a mother she cannot help fearing for the safety of her only child. She did not wish to talk to her husband about her anxiety, though, because even though he did not forbid his daughter to participate in the protests, as a government official, Nasser is not too supportive of these protests.

Fatemeh finished her cooking and came to the balcony. Her neighbours are enjoying family dinner in their courtyard. Fatemeh smiled and waved at them. The night sky, now a deep indigo, is dotted with stars, creating a peaceful canopy over the suburbs. The clock is showing eight-thirty. Fatemeh went to her husband and said, "Nasser, Sara is still not home. Should we call her friends?"

Nasser Ali put the newspaper aside, looked at the wall clock, frowned, shook his head and said, "I told you both not to get involved in this protest nonsense. Did you listen to me?"

"What have I done now, Nasser? It's your daughter who wanted to go there. And it is a good thing, you know, all her friends are also going. The way they killed that girl, Masha. She is as old as our Sara, just imagine what her parents must be going through," Fatemeh reasoned.

"Look Fatemeh, I have full sympathy for this girl, Masha Amini. What they did to her is not right. But the governor has apologized, what else do you expect them to do? They cannot bring the girl back, can they? And all these protests... US and other Western countries are fuelling this, I am telling you, they are using our gullible youths and they are playing right into their hands—"

Fatemeh's phone rang before her husband could finish his rant. It was Zeinab, Sara's friend. She picked it up quickly. But a minute into the call, her face turned ashen.

"What happened, Fatemeh?" Nasser was worried.

"Nasser... it is Sara... she, she is in the hospital." Fatemeh was shaking.

"Hospital? What for? What happened? Any accident?"

Nasser held his wife to prevent her from falling.

"P-Police, they came to disperse the protesters. A few in the front line were badly beaten. Sara... our Sara..." Fatemeh could not finish her sentence as her voice choked.

## Alpha Beta Gamma

Nasser and Fatemeh Ali rushed to the hospital immediately. But they never saw their daughter alive again. After waiting for two agonizing hours in the waiting room full of other anxious parents and relatives, they were finally shown the body of Sara. The white bedsheet was stained with blood, their only child's blood. Nasser let out a cry, but Fatemeh was silent. She never spoke a word after that, until the day of Sara's funeral.

Nasser on the other hand, was calling people fanatically. His boss, his colleagues, the government officials. He knows a lot of them, high up in the ministry. How could they do this to him? Him, a loyal employee, serving his government and his country for so many years, often taking huge, personal risks. All his sacrifices, his loyalty, don't they have any value?

"Look, Nasser, I feel your pain, I really do. I knew Sara since she was little, she is like my own child. But what can one do? When God wants someone dead…"

Nasser's boss, Arash Ahmed, spoke as he put his arms around Nasser's shoulder to console him after Sara's funeral.

"No, Sir, God did not want my child dead. It was the morality police. They killed her, savagely beat her to death. How can this happen in a civilized country, sir? Ours is one of the oldest civilizations, what has happened to us?"

"Now, Nasser, I know you are grieving, but please do not parrot those words of the US imperialists. I do not want to blame you, but you should have prevented Sara from joining those protests."

"Sir! It was a peaceful protest. They were just a bunch of kids, University students, unarmed. How can you kill them like this?"

"Sometimes these seemingly peaceful protests cause more damage than a few armed thugs. You should know better, Nasser. The whole international media is covering it, dragging our reputation into the mud. You know how it works, Nasser. Sometimes these things happen, unintentionally, to serve a greater cause. What do they call it in English? Collateral Damage, right?"

Nasser did not say anything more. His eyes shifted from his stone-faced wife to the big, lively photo of his only daughter... the collateral damage. He has given all his adult life to serve this country. Not even his immediate family knows what he actually does for a living, they think that he is in the police. But he is not a regular police officer. He works for the secret police; he is a spy. Throughout his career, he has taken numerous risks to fulfil his duty. He has always dutifully treated the sensitive state information as sacred secrets. He has declined offers of huge bribes by the foreign agencies to act as a double agent. They call him Iranian 007 for a reason. And what does he get in return? Collateral damage.

## Alpha Beta Gamma

Alright then, if he is on his own, then he will do whatever is necessary to provide justice for his murdered daughter, thought Nasser Ali, as he was looking at the starry night sky, when everyone had gone home after the funeral. Arash Ahmed has no idea what Nasser is capable of. He has troves of top-secret information which, until now, he has always treated as sacred. But not any longer.

As he looked above, a shooting star quickly streaked past across the Orion constellation. Nasser took this as a good omen, almost a nod from his dead daughter to go ahead with his idea.

That night, he devised a clear and meticulous plan. He will get hold of the most damaging information, which will show many atrocities that this government has committed, but which no one could ever prove. Now they will have proof, lethal proof. Nasser will have to send them to some western news agency, either in the US or in Europe.

But he cannot contact the news agencies directly, that will be too much of a risk. He doesn't care for his own safety anymore, but he has to protect Fatemeh, his mother, his whole extended family. So, he has to use an intermediary.

He has such a person in mind. A University professor in London. The professor is of Iranian ancestry, but had fled the country almost thirty years back. But he still remains very critical of the government here and is also a vocal supporter of these protests against the morality police. He also wrote a strong post, accusing the government of murder after Sara's death. Nasser doesn't know him yet, their political views are world apart, but he can contact him. If he introduces himself as Sara's father, then surely this professor will agree to help him. He may even suggest Nasser the best news outlet to contact.

Very well then, this will be Nasser's mission now. Arash said Sara's peaceful protest was dragging the country's reputation to mud. Now they will get a taste of what dragging the reputation to mud actually looks like, when they are charged with war crimes by the UN.

It will be a difficult mission, but Nasser Ali will have to do it. He owes it to Fatemeh, he owes it to Sara.

Alpha Beta Gamma

## *Murder In The Lab*

Beep… Beep…Beep…

The shrill sound of my alarm jolted me awake, and I groaned, slapping at my phone to silence the noise. My eyes felt heavy, gritty with the remnants of sleep deprivation. I had stayed up way too late last night, cramming for that quantum mechanics exam.

The clock on my nightstand blinked 6:30 AM in harsh red digits, reminding me that I had an 8 AM class.

With a sigh, I dragged myself out of bed, my muscles protesting every movement. The cool air of the room hit me, and I shivered, pulling my blanket tighter around me as I shuffled to the bathroom. My reflection in the mirror looked as tired as I felt. Dark circles under my eyes, hair a tangled mess. I splashed cold water on my face, hoping it would wake me up, but it barely made a dent in my exhaustion.

Hastily putting on some clothes — sweatpants and a hoodie, the uniform of the chronically sleep deprived student — I headed to the kitchen. I fumbled with the coffee maker, waiting impatiently as it dripped hot, freshly brewed Illy coffee into my mug. I sipped it gratefully, feeling the caffeine slowly start to clear the fog in my brain.

I really needed to hurry up now, otherwise, there would be no chance in hell of me making to the Mathematical Physics class on TIME. Professor Yunis does not like students coming late to his class. 'If you can't make it on time then please don't bother coming at all, it just disturbs my teaching rhythm,' he made himself quite clear at the beginning of his course.

For the last couple of weeks now I have been managing with just five or six hours of sleep. This, unfortunately, is quite a normal routine, right before these end-of-term exams. Though mum always says, 'Such last-minute crazy cramming is futile, Sri, as futile as the deathbed confessions of lifelong sinners.'

"Morning, Sri!"

## Alpha Beta Gamma

My flatmate, Mathew Holmes, aka Matt is up already. This is his flat. I am just renting a room here. He owns a business, some kind of an agency near the Tower Bridge. Matt is strikingly handsome — six feet two with an athletic build, strong jawline, a headful of light brown hair and a pair of clear blue eyes. No wonder my friends Samapti and Riddhima have expressed their desire to "devour" him after seeing his photo in the social media.

I am not extrovert like them. I am a bespectacled, bookish, introvert girl. However, that does not stop me from quietly admiring such an exquisite piece of male beauty. Honestly, I have a huge crush on him. From day one. I do put in a lot of effort to hide it. Not sure if it works very well, though. I suspect that Matt is aware of my crush. But even if he is, he does not show it. Matt is a perfect gentleman and is always very polite and friendly with me. He does not have a steady girlfriend. To quote him, he is still 'playing the field.' Almost every weekend, I meet a new girl in our kitchen or living room.

Anyway, neither Matt nor his girlfriends are the source of my biggest worry right now. I have a handful of other things to think about. First, I have three pending assignments which are due by Friday. Second, it seems all my data from the diffraction pattern experiment are wrong; they are producing some very weird looking graphs, which indicates that I have to re-do the experiment. Third, we have to arrange a surprise party for Sahil's upcoming birthday. The last and the trickiest one is that I have to visit Aunt Shukla this weekend.

Aunt Shukla is mum's second cousin. We were never that close to her, but as soon as I got the offer from the Queen Mary College to do my masters, mum called her and implored her to be the local guardian of her hopeless, naive daughter, me. Obviously, I asked mum why a twenty-three-year-old woman need any guardian, local or global.
'Don't try to act smart Sri. You will be all alone in a foreign land. It always helps to have a family member nearby,' was mum's curt reply.

Aunt Shukla does not live nearby, though. She lives in Wimbledon, which is neither close to my college nor to my apartment in Canning Town. It takes about an hour and a half of toil in the underground to reach there. Moreover, twenty-five years of expat life have transformed Aunt Shukla and her family into a strange hotchpotch which is neither fully British nor fully Indian.

## Alpha Beta Gamma

She has two children, who speak no Bengali. They have a cockney accent, they listen to Taylor Swift and watch EastEnders or Love Island on the telly, yet they are forbidden to date anyone other than a pukka Bengali-Indian. Aunt Shukla has a busy social life. She is actively engaged in various community organizations, like the Putney Puja committee and the Wimbledon Bengali Association. Her husband, uncle Pavitro works as an accountant and is a member of the local Tory party. They always talk about privatizing; railways, banks, the NHS everything, for the sake of bringing 'economic prosperity' and 'operating efficiency'. How come, then, the failed banks had to be bailed out with public money? No answer to such inconvenient 'lefty' questions, obviously!

That is why, despite their immaculate house, tidy garden, delicious food and generous hospitality, I absolutely loathe visiting them.

'You cannot be such a social misfit all the time, Sri!' mum cautioned me. Though, I distinctly remember that, back in Kolkata, she was the one who used to complain about my 'too busy social life', which apparently was hindering my possibility of getting even better grades. But I know it is futile to point it out; inconsistency thy name is mum!

"Sri, don't forget your keys!" Matt reminds me. For very good reason, actually. I forgot my keys last Friday and was locked out. Matt was out with his date in Ealing. I had no other option but to call him. He came to my rescue in the middle of the night. It was so embarrassing! No wonder my best friend Samapti calls me sloppy.

The train is now approaching Mile End station. It's ten minutes to eight. Shit! I would be a few minutes late. Prof. Yunis will not be very happy. I start running.

I am stopped abruptly at the entrance of our department building. Panting, I look around. The whole place is cordoned off with yellow police ribbons. Startled, I look around. A handful of people with very serious faces are standing nearby. There are two police cars parked on the curb. Through the glass doors, I can see more police officers inside. A couple of them are in hazmat suits.

What on earth is going on?

As I look around, I see my classmates, Sadia, Louis, and Ed, are standing on the other side of the pavement. I go to them and whisper, "What happened?"

"It's Professor Tavacol." Louis whispers back.

"Who? Reza Tavacol? Condensed Matter?" I ask to double check.

Sadia nods to confirm.

"What happened?" I ask again.

"Don' know… but I think he is dead." Ed replies hesitantly.

"Dead? How?"

"No one knows." Sadia replies solemnly.

"Martha, the condensed matter lab assistant, came in the morning and opened the door and found Reza lying on his back on the floor. Looked like he'd been dead for hours."

"Then?" I gasp.

"Then what? Martha screams.

"Then more people came running, someone called 999, then police, ambulance…" Sadia paints a brief but clear picture.

"There won't be any class today, I suppose?" I ask again after a pause.

"No. Prof Yunis just told us. He is also the dean of physical sciences, isn't he? He needs to be with the police now." Ed is right.

"Let's go to the cafeteria. We can talk there."

Everyone seems to agree, and we silently march towards the cafeteria.

"Really, I can't believe this! Who would kill a professor in his own lab?" I ask, sipping my latte.

"Hold on a sec, who told you it's a murder?" asks Ed, frowning.

"What else? I mean, like this… out of the blue…"

"Could very well be a cardiac arrest. There hasn't been any autopsy yet." Louis interjects.

"Yeah, but…"

"You wouldn't like a cardiac arrest, would you?" Sadia smiled.

"Oh, yeah, of course, how can I forget? Our Miss Sherlock Holmes." Louis comments.

"No, no… Miss Marple." Ed corrects him.

"Nah, Ms. Marple is too old. Lara Croft." Now it's Sadia's turn to pull my leg.

"All wrong. Lara is female Indiana Jones, not a detective. Old lady Miss Marple knits and gossips and Mr. Holmes takes cocaine and smokes a pipe. I am nothing like any one of them." I protest firmly.

"Humm. Any Indian detectives? From Bengali literature?" Sadia enquires.

"There are plenty. But all are male, living in an alternate universe where women are practically invisible," I reply bluntly.

"Jesus! Even in 2023?" Luis seems genuinely surprised.

"Of course. And it will continue to be so for eternity."

"What if anyone dares to break the mould?"

"Then she or he will be thoroughly persecuted and hounded. Will be virtually hanged by the culture police on social media!"

"I see! So not so pale, but male and stale, right?" Ed seems to have gotten the gist of it.

"Precisely!" I agree.

# Alpha Beta Gamma

All my friends know about my obsession with crime fiction, and it is a constant theme for them to pull my leg. But I know very well that being a detective is quite different from liking detective stories. I have zero observational power. I always lose things; books, pens, chargers, keys, everything. I hold the world record in losing brollies. Unlike the famous fictional detectives, I cannot deduce what someone had eaten for the supper last night, what the colour of their toothbrush is, or where the ex-girlfriend of their second cousin lives, just by looking at someone for the fraction of a second.

On the contrary, I forget people's names, overlook the most obvious things. I do not know any martial arts or how to use a gun. In a nutshell, I am rather ill-equipped to be a sleuth.

But that of course does not mean that I am not curious. I am a physicist. It is our job to unveil the mysteries of the universe. I have to be curious. And now, I am curious to know who killed our friendly, middle aged, Professor Reza Tavacol in his own lab.

Sadia and Ed go to the library to finish the pending assignments. Although I also need to work on them, I did not want to feel like a third wheel. Ed and Sadia have just started going out, but they have not told many people about it yet. I suspect it is because of Sadia's family. Hers is a very conservative Pakistani family and if they get even a whiff of it, it will be a big trouble. They want to marry her off to her cousin in Karachi.

Louis goes to the gym. He is a fitness freak, always doing something, running, or swimming or lifting weights. A few others from my class have come to the cafeteria now. I think of joining them for a moment, but then go outside instead.

As I step out of the cafeteria onto the cobblestone pathway, a crisp November breeze greets me, carrying the earthy scent of fallen leaves. The sky is a patchwork of grey clouds, but occasional streaks of sunlight are breaking through, casting a soft glow on the University buildings around me. I pull my scarf tighter around my neck and begin my walk through the campus.

The trees lining the pathway are nearly bare, their last few yellow and orange leaves clinging stubbornly to the branches. The sound of my footsteps mingles with the rustling leaves underfoot, creating a soothing rhythm as I make my way towards our department. I pass by the central fountain, where the water is still running, though the surface is dotted with fallen leaves. With my hands in my pocket, I continue on, crossing the main courtyard.

Our building is at the edge of the campus, and I can already hear the bustling streets outside. Soon I find myself in front of our department's main door again.

"Could I go in for a sec? I left my laptop charger inside." I ask the police officer guarding the door.

"ID?" He asks coldly. I show him my ID.

"Which floor?" Asks the officer, returning my ID.

"Second floor. That room over there, in the corner. Room number two-hundred and eleven." I reply, pointing towards our classroom upstairs.

"Alright. You can go in there. But don't go towards the ground floor corridor, it's cordoned off."

"I see. So, no chance of going to the condensed matter lab then? Reza's lab?"

"No," the officer replies sternly.

I go inside and, as I start climbing up the stairs, I glance at the ground floor corridor. It is indeed cordoned off. The Spectroscopy lab is right beside Reza's. I do not think anyone can go in there either.

It is true that I need my charger. But I also have a strong urge to have a quick look at Reza's lab. Don't know why though. Maybe my friends are right, I am obsessed with crime mysteries. Perhaps I should stop—

My thoughts came to a jolting halt as I bump straight into someone coming hurriedly down the stairs.

"Sorry!" we both say simultaneously.

Who is he? No one I know from our department. He is not in a police uniform either. A new face during this conundrum? That is fishy, very fishy.

"Are you a student here?" the man asks me, before I could ask him anything.

"Yes. But you?"

"Where were you going?" he asks again, without answering my question.

"To my classroom."

"Which class? What's the room number?"

"Theoretical Physics class. Room number 211." I start getting annoyed by his interrogation.

"What time is your class? All classes have been dismissed until lunch. Don't you know that?"

"I know. But I left my laptop charger there yesterday. I need it now."

"Hmm. What is your name?"

"Srija Ray. Masters, third semester. Who are you? Why are you interrogating me like this? How did you even get in here? Do the police know?" I blurt out.

"Neil Basu, Met Police." He shows his badge with a faint smile on his lips.

Wow, is he a police officer? But why is he not in uniform then?

Did he just say he surname is Basu? Is he Bengali?

"Are you Bengali?" I ask in Bengali.

"Sorry?" He seems a little startled.

"I am sorry! I thought you might be a Bengali, like me, your surname …" I return to English.

"Oh, I see! Don't worry, I get that a lot. My father is Bengali, but mum is Scottish. I was born and brought up here and my Bengali knowledge is close to zero." He smiles.

I see. So, he is like my cousins, Riju and Rikta, Aunt Shukla's children. Perhaps he is even less Bengali than they are, given his mum is British. That possibly explains his features: hazel eyes and chestnut brown hair. Good height, too. Six-one? Or two?

"Did you know Professor Tavacol?"

Another question. This man could be a quizmaster for the rapid-fire round.

"Of course I knew him! Why shouldn't I? He used to teach us the phase transition in condensed matter theory. I also did experiments in his lab. I thought of doing my thesis with him in the final semester."

"Really? Thesis on what, exactly?"

Now this really irritates me to death. What does this arrogant prick think of himself? Will he be able to understand my thesis topic even if I tell him? Being a police officer doesn't make him de-facto know it all.

"I was thinking of doing some experiments on quantum magnetism and quantum phase transition."

"I see. Using neutron scattering?"

Wow, I didn't see this coming! Seems he is not totally ignorant in Physics.

"Y-Yes, something like that. What is your background, by the way?" I ask.

"Why? Did you think all policemen are dumb? Just muscles, no brains?" He smirks.

"N-no, I didn't mean that, obviously. I mean police will be police, right? They are not expected to be scientists, right? For that—"

"—For that there are smart people like you, right? Don't worry, I am not after your job. But I did study Physics at Uni, hence I happen to know a thing or two about the subject. Perhaps that is why they sent me here."

"Why? Is there a physics connection with Professor Tavacol's murder?" I am curious.

"Ms Ray! I never said Reza was murdered!" Neil Basu is smiling, but his voice is sharp.

"Sorry, I may have used a wrong term. I am not a police officer, you see! So, I do not know all the technicalities here. But it is an unnatural death, right?"

"Not sure. It could be a cardiac arrest, too. We have not done any postmortem yet."

"This many police officers for a cardiac arrest? In hazmat suits? Met Police? MI5?"

"MI5? Who? James Bond?"

"No. You!"

"Ms. Ray, you are new in this country. So perhaps you don't know it, MI5 is not the Met Police."

"I know that."

"When did you last change your glasses?"

"Last year, and my eyesight is fine. Are you talking about your badge which you just showed? That must be fake."

"Fake? Fake police badge?"

"Well, maybe you are not actually in the Met Police!" I smile.

"What's your point? Do you even have one?"

"Yes, I do. I think you are actually from MI5, and they gave you this fake badge, to disguise your true identity. They do that, right? James Bond has so many identities…"

"Wow! Look, Ms. Ray, I am flattered that a beautiful girl like you mistook me for James Bond, but—"

"On duty flirting with potential witness. A Met police officer would never do that. But a MI5 spy can."

"You are clever!"

"Yes, I am. Otherwise I would not get a full scholarship to do a Masters in physics here. What is your suspicion? Radiation poisoning? Like Litvinenko? At the Sushi Bar in 2006?"

"My, my! Ms. Ray…"

"Call me Sri, Mr. Basu."

"Well, Sri, why radiation poisoning, all of a sudden? Do you watch a lot of spy thrillers?"

"Yes, I do watch a lot of spy thrillers. But that is not why I am suspecting radiation poisoning. It is because of that thing in your hand."

I pointed towards the small bag in Neil's hand.

"This? What—?"

"I mean the Geiger Counter that you are carrying in that bag. MI5, physics background. You are the right man to carry a Geiger Counter, aren't you?"

"Unbelievable! Slight correction though, I work in MI6. Are you interested in joining us?"

"Are you offering me job?" I am taken aback.

"We always need young, talented people."

"You are young, talented. I don't want a career in crime."

"Sri, it is called a career *against* crime, not *in* crime. Anyway, perhaps by now you have understood that you cannot go to your classroom just yet. Soon your dean will email you all regarding the alternate classrooms."

"Shit!"

"What is the big deal? You just have to do your classes in a different building for a while."

"What about the labs? More than half of our work is in the labs, Mr. Basu, you should know, being a physics major yourself."

"Yes, I know. But we can't do anything about it, unfortunately. I'm sorry. This is a question of security for all students and faculties. Are all your labs here in this building?" Neil asks.

"Well, most of them are. The spectroscopy lab is right beside Reza's. I need to re-do the diffraction pattern experiment. The last one is producing shitty curves."

"Well, you can't do it right now, I am afraid. Anyway, I must leave now, but before that, could you please give me your number?"

"I don't give my number to strangers."

"That's good, but I'm not asking you out. You've got to give it to Police if they ask."

"I wouldn't mind if you asked me out—" Neil gives me a piercing look. I feel so angry with myself. It came out all wrong, that's not what I meant, really! "— But you are not. Why then do you need my number? Am I a suspect? Do I carry radioactive substances in my pocket?"

"First of all, we don't know yet if it is radioactive poisoning or not. Could be some other nerve agent or poison, too. And second of all, not everyone is a suspect but many of them can be witnesses. You were Professor Tavacol's student, knew him well, so you are a valuable witness."

"But that's true for everyone in our class. Will you take their phone numbers, too?"

"Everyone is not Ms. Marple, are they?" Neil smiles.

"I am not Ms. Marple. I will never be a detective. I always lose things, keys, chargers…"

"Hmm. Maybe you should get a detective partner. Who can find the stuffs you keep losing!"

"Are you hitting on me?"

"No. Phone number, please."

Just as Neil Basu is leaving after taking my number, I speak again,

"Listen…"

"Yes…?"

"I mean, can I get your number please?"

"Why? Do you want to ask me out?"

"Ha-Ha! Very funny! I wanted it because… I mean… if I remember something later on… about Prof. Tavacol, I mean …" I stammer.

"Then you should inform your dean. He will let me know. Bye."


So rude! He took my number but refused to give me his.

"*Paji*" I mumble in Bengali. It means scoundrel.

"What did you say?" Neil heard it.

"Nothing!"

"No. You said *paji*, didn't you? I know this much Bengali."

"No, you heard it wrong." I lied.

"Don't think so! Anyway, listen, if you really want to go on a date with me, then I will be happy to give you my private number. But I have to be a bit cautious about sharing my work number, for obvious reasons. Hope you understand."

"Yes, I understand. Bye."

"Do you want my private number?"

"No. Save it for somebody else. I don't go on dates."

"Why? Do you have a boyfriend at home?"

"No."

"Girlfriend?"

"No."

"Then?"

"It is my choice!"

## *The Sloppy Sleuth*

I came home after seven that evening. The entire day had been a colossal waste. Everyone was still reeling from the shocking death of prof. Tavacol. All classes were cancelled. Labs on the ground floor of our building were all sealed. A bunch of people in hazmat suits were running around with Geiger Counters in their hands. Everyone was freaking out and the gossip mill was running overtime. We all gathered at the foyer in the afternoon, and everyone had with their own opinion in this matter.

"Well, Reza is originally from Iran. Perhaps that explains it," Louis commented.

"So what? Are all Iranians spies?" retorted Mohammad. He is also from Iran.

"That's not what I meant. But perhaps Reza had enemies there. Political or other enemies."

"What were they doing all these years? He'd been living here for more than thirty years now."

"Well, maybe they didn't get the opportunity before. What do you think, Sri? Does it sound like a probable cause? Political persecution or an old grudge?" Louis asked me.

Instead of answering Louis, I asked a different question, "Do you know anything about Reza's family?"

Everyone fell silent. Amongst all these conspiracy theories, gossips and rumours we almost forgot about the real victim. Prof Reza Tavacol. Aged fifty-seven. PhD from Cambridge, Post Doc from Rutgers. Has been teaching at Queen Mary for the last twenty-five years. Published about two hundred scientific papers in various prestigious journals, including Nature, Science and Phys-Rev Letters. A friendly, well liked, decent guy. Lived in Islington for the last twenty years. Why would such a man be killed one day in his own lab? What must his family be going through right now? For whom he is not just a tagged body in a morgue or a sensational news, but a father or husband or brother?

Perhaps similar thoughts had crossed others' minds, too, because suddenly all became very quiet and then dispersed shortly afterwards.

I stood there for a few more minutes thinking what to do now. Since the spectroscopy lab was inaccessible, I headed for the library to work on the assignments. Then I went down to the IT department for a replacement charger. Afterwards, we all went to Covent Garden to buy a birthday gift for Sahil.

Finally, when I get home, I'm feeling quite tired. The lights in the living room and kitchen are on, indicating Matt was home already. As I crush into the sofa, the bathroom door across the corridor opens and Matt steps out of it. He has just finished showering. He is wearing just a white towel, his upper body bare. A combined fragrance of shampoo, cologne and aftershave fills the room. His ripped body, his dense, slightly wet, light brown hair… I force myself to look elsewhere. He should not get the impression that I am ogling at him.

"Hi Sri! When did you come back?" Smiles Matt, showing his perfect teeth.
"Just now."
"Any plans for dinner?"
He is now standing very close to me, really close. A few drops of water are rolling slowly down his ripped chest, the fragrance of Hugo Boss aftershave is stirring my senses… impossible! It is torture.
I get up from the sofa and head straight to the open plan kitchen.
"No, I don't have any plans. Feeling a bit tired, actually. Was thinking of making some egg and toast." I reply, without looking at him.
"Egg and toast for dinner! Are you alright?"
He is again standing too close, right behind me. I am not looking at him, but I can smell his fragrance, can even feel his warm breath at my neck.

"Yeah, I am fine. Just very tired." I move away from the kitchen.

"Had a tough day, did you?"

"Yeah, kind of! You know, one of our professors seems to have been murdered. In his own lab, can you believe? Then all our classes were cancelled… police, ambulance… such a mess!"

"Oh, my, my! Sri, please go and have a shower, you will feel so much better. I'll make dinner for both of us. Baked salmon pasta. Will that do?"

"No, Matt, really, don't bother. I'll make something simple for me."

"No Sri, do as I say! I was going to make it for myself anyway. Making it for two instead is not a big hassle. It is the same amount of effort, really. I have got good Bordeaux. Let's have a candlelight dinner at home. It will be ready by the time you finish showering."

"What's the matter Matt? Don't you have any lady friend tonight?" I smile.

"Well, I have you! Both a lady and a friend!" He smiles back charmingly.

Matt has always been very nice and friendly towards me. But never this chatty or flirty! I could not understand what has happened all of a sudden. Anyway, I can't think about it right now. I am going to get a readymade lovely dinner soon. That's all that counts.

When I get back to the living room after taking the shower, I see that the lights are all dimmed. Matt has not only finished cooking, but he has also arranged the table nicely, complete with three big candles and a single carnation in an empty glass jar. The appetizing aroma of baked salmon pasta fills the apartment. It is so much better than my original plan of having toast and egg in my room.

"So, one of your professors has been murdered, has he?" asks Matt, pouring the wine into our glasses. He is now wearing regular track pants and T-Shirt. But I can't help picturing his ripped chest and the lion-like narrow waist right under those plain clothes.

"Yeah, it seems so" I reply absentmindedly.

"Who would have thought?!"

"Sorry?"

"I mean a professor at Uni is considered to be one of the safest jobs on Earth. Getting murdered there is a bit shocking, don't you think?"

I keep eating without saying anything.

"How was he killed? Stabbing? Or gunshot?"

"No… I think radio— I mean poisoning."

"Poison? Cyanide? Or…?"

"I don't know. I think we will only know for sure after the autopsy."

I honestly do not want to have this discussion now. In college, we talked about this morbid stuff the whole day today. Now I really don't want to think about it anymore.

"Will the police question all of you?" Matt is still curious.

"They will question the dean and the other academics, for sure. But I don't think they will interrogate all the students. That's impossible, really."

"I see. So, you didn't have to talk to the police then?"

Momentarily, Neil Basu's face flashes through my mind. But I reply, "No. Can you give me the recipe for this? It's delicious."

"It is very simple. I'll show you. So, you will resume your regular classes from tomorrow then, right?"

"No. All classes have been suspended for the rest of the week. They have sealed the building."

"Strange! Why would a single murder cause the entire building to be sealed?"

Matt should have worked in police. Or in MI6. Perhaps I should introduce him to Mr. Basu. He is looking for young, talented recruits anyway. They would get along well, I suppose. Both are roughly of the same age, both are quite handsome... God! why am I now thinking of Neil Basu? Just a while back I was ogling at Matt and now I am musing over 'handsome' Neil. What has happened to me? Am I ovulating or what?

"So, why is the whole building sealed?" Matt keeps pressing.

"I don't know Matt, perhaps you should ask Neil Basu."

"Who?"

"Neil Basu. He came to investigate. I spoke to him briefly. Perhaps he can give you all the details."

"So, you did speak to the Met police then!" Matt smiles.

"No, Neil is in MI6."

"What? MI6? Why? Do they suspect terrorism?"

"Don't know."

"The professor, who was murdered, did he by chance have any Russian or North Korean connection?"

"No. He was Iranian."

"I see! But why did MI6 speak to you? Were you very close to that deceased professor?"

"No. I ran into the officer rather accidentally. We bumped into each other on the stairs."

"You are saying it was neither stabbing nor gunshot, and MI6 is already involved. Could it be radiation poisoning?"

"Why would you say that, Matt?" I'm intrigued.

"Don't know. Just thought of it. Could be because of my background, you see. I have a Masters in Chemistry."

Matt smiled charmingly.

"Really? Didn't know that! What is your alma matter?"

"Cambridge."

"Wow! You are a real scholar then! Why didn't you go into academia then?"

"Never fancied academia. My interest lies elsewhere." He smiles again.

"Where?" I enquire.

"That's a long story, I will tell you some day. But tell me one thing now, were there people in hazmat suits in your college today? Near the murder spot?"

"I… I don't remember."

I took a couple of large gulps from my wine glass. I seriously begin to think that Matt's curiosity in this murder is way above normal.

"Hey, Sri! What are you doing? Don't drink so fast. You'll get drunk." Smiling, Matt cautions me. But I don't reply.

"Sorry, my fault. I am stressing you out by talking so much about it. Let's talk about other things."

We change the subject and over the next forty minutes we have a lovely dinner discussing Kohli's batting, Labour party infighting, the state of the NHS, the climate crisis, and many other things. Matt is indeed a good company; witty, with a fantastic sense of humour and healthy interest in a great many things.

It's only nine thirty when I go to my room after cleaning up. But I am feeling exhausted already. Just as I switch off the bedside lamp, a thought suddenly crosses my mind: how would Neil look in a white towel?

Oh God, I need therapy! I rolled over and close my eyes.

***

Aunt Shukla's four-bedroom detached house in the leafy suburb of Wimbledon is teeming with guests today. Most of them are Indians but there are a handful of others as well. All guests are dressed in expensive clothes, came in expensive cars. Aunt Shukla is a generous hostess, offering a variety of delicious dishes; seventeen items, not including the desserts, aunty Shukla boasted a while ago. Their house is spacious, with a beautifully landscaped garden in the upscale area of Wimbledon, known for its quiet streets adorned with lush greenery.

Had I known it would be such a big affair, I would have made some excuse and skipped it. My aunt and uncle alone are a handful to take on, and today they have the whole gang. Women have gathered in the dining hall and are taking group selfies. Soon they will post hundreds of very similar photos in their Facebook, spamming everyone in their contact lists. Men, sitting in two reception rooms are discussing right wing politics. Small children are playing outside in the garden. A handful of thoroughly bored teenagers are engrossed in their mobile phones. Feeling like a big misfit everywhere, I sit on the stairs and start browsing through my phone.

"Sri! What are you doing here with your phone? Do you Facebook all the time?" Aunt Shukla has found me.

Facebook! Who does that? Isn't that for the people born in the last century? Where people post pictures of their dinner dishes, family holidays and kitchen herbs? She could have said Snap, TikTok or at least Insta! I don't even have a Facebook account, for God's sake!

"Come with me... I will introduce you to my friends."

I had to follow my aunt to her friends in the dining hall.

"This is my niece, Srija. She is doing a Masters at Queen Mary. In Physics." Aunty sounds rather proud.

"My nephew joined Oxford last year," sneers the plump woman in the pink sari.

"Your nephew is studying Sociology, isn't he, Sheila? Physics is way more difficult than that," Aunt Shukla snaps back.

"Physics has no future these days."

The wise comment comes from the lady sitting at the corner, holding a glass of orange juice in her hand.

(Oh dear! Poor Physics! Despite being there since the Big Bang, you have just been made redundant today in Aunt Shukla's dining room.)

"So true! That is why my sister-in-law sent her son to MIT to study computer science," agrees the woman in the figure-hugging cocktail dress.

"Isn't this the same sister-in-law whom you absolutely despise, Prachi? How come you suddenly feel proud of her son?" Aunt Shukla doesn't mince her words. "Sri is very sharp. Especially in math and science. After the Masters, she will do research in condensed milk."

"Aunty!!! It's condensed matter not condensed milk!" I scream in horror.

"It's all the same, darling, milk is also a matter, is it not?"

Aunt Shukla is not easily perturbed.

"Where are you studying? At Imperial?" asks the lady in white salwar who just entered the room. She has very little make up on and her smile looks authentic.

"No. At Queen Mary," my aunt corrects her.

"Oh, I see! Didn't one of your professors get murdered recently? Saw it on the news," the white salwar asks.

"Really? Murder? On the campus?" Pink sari seems curious.

"Is it? In your department? What was his name?" the lady with the orange juice questions.

"Yes, in our department. Professor Reza Tavacol," I reply.

"Reza? Pakistani?" Pink Sari's nose twitches a little.

"See, these are the problems with these colleges... they do not get good faculty, you see! It's not like that at MIT. They only have good white professors." The cocktail dress made the abhorrent, racist comment in a very nonchalant way.

"No, that's not true!" I blurt out loudly. Everyone falls silent, even Aunt Shukla.

"You have no idea what you are talking about. MIT is full of foreign-origin faculty. It's the same in all ivy league colleges, Harvard, Yale, Columbia. I know it. I have friends and collaborators there. You can verify it on their websites if you like."

Everyone is still silent. Before leaving the room, I turn back again and made my final remark, "Reza was Iranian. A Cambridge PhD. A Rutgers postdoc. One of the finest professors in condensed matter physics. His papers were published in journals like Nature and Science. Any ivy league would have been fortunate to have him."

I go outside and sit on a bench in the garden. Thank heavens that mum is not here. She would have gone ballistic for my outburst 'disrespecting the elders.' No matter how unreasonable the 'elders' are, you are not supposed to contradict them. That's mum's philosophy, not mine though.

"Here... you left it in there." The white salwar is standing in front of me with my glass of coke in her hand.

"Thanks!" I take the glass from her.
"No worries. What is your name?"
"Sri."
"Sree? That's lovely! Very apt for a beautiful girl like you." She gives me a sweet smile.

*Sree* means beauty in Bengali, hence her comment.

"It's not Sree. It's Sri… Srija." I correct her. A lot of people make the same mistake.

"I see. I am Suparna."
"Nice to meet you."
"You are very angry with them, aren't you?" She sits beside me. I don't reply. I am in no mood for small talk right now.

"Can't blame you, though! You see, most of them were mediocre students. Somehow bagged a successful husband to come here. They are not self-made, like you!"

"They can do whatever fuck they want to do, I don't care."

(Mum would surely have killed me if she heard.)

"But if they talk about things they have no idea of, and insult others, I'll not let them off easily. Racist, xenophobic bitches." I let it all out.

"Language, Sri!"

Suparna warns me, just like mum.

"What language, Suparna? They have no respect for a deceased man. Reza was my professor, my mentor. I used to meet him daily for work. He was so kind, helpful, a perfect gentleman…" my voice starts cracking.

"Where did he live?" asks Suparna, handing me a tissue.

"Islington." I wipe my nose.

"Oh! I also live there. You will go there to visit his family, won't you? Why don't you come over to my place, too?"

From our class we were planning to visit Reza's widow, but we have not fixed any date yet.

"You must visit North London, you see! Otherwise, you will have a very wrong impression of London. You would think it is only about tasteless show-offs and the stupid bragging of the wealthy suburbs."

"Is it not?" I finally smile.

"No, absolutely not. London is not just about the cold, calculating financial districts of the City or the snooty, super riches of Chelsea. It also has the liberal and cultural heart of Islington," Suparna smiles back.

"What do you do for a living?" I ask.

"I work in cyber security. I am an ethical hacker."

"Wow! That sounds awesome! Now I am getting even more intrigued to visit you."

"Please do come! I can't promise you seventeen dishes like Shukla, but I do have tons of books."

Books! My greatest weakness. Suparna has put the right bait for me. She is a clever lady, indeed.

"Well, then I will definitely go! Who do you have in your family?"

"I don't have a big family. It's just me and my partner, Aniket Basu."

"What does your partner do? Is he also in cyber security?"

"Oh, No! Aniket is a doctor. Cardiologist. It is just two of us at home. Though Aniket's son, Neil, visits us occasionally. Take my number…"

So, instead of Neil's I now get his stepmum's number. Wicked!

\*\*\*

"Finally! They have opened the classrooms again." Sadia sounds relieved as we all sit round the big table at our campus cafeteria.

"Really, how did you survive the last week? Without the classes, must have been so darn hard for you. Could you even breathe?" Dave asks sarcastically.

"They didn't cancel the exams, did they? How does cancelling the classes just before the exam help anyone?" Sadia retorts back.

"What's the big deal? You will get slightly lower grades. Not the end of the world!" shrugs Dave.

"No Dave, you don't get it. We are Asians. Bad grades are not an option for us. I am Chinese, Sadia is Pakistani, Sri is Indian, and we all know it." Louis explains and we all nod.

"Fuck! Aren't you all British?" Dave frowns.

"Of course. I was talking of ethnicity," Louis replies.

"Not me. I am Indian. Both by ethnicity and by nationality. I am not a colonizer." I comment.

"Fuck man! British colonies were not that bad." Dave is trying to provoke us.

"Trust me, it was bad. Pretty bad." I cut him short.

"I agree." Sadia.

"Me too." Louis.

"I also agree." Mike. He is from Jamaica.

"I agree too. And I am ashamed of it." Ed. Even though he is native British.

"Traitor!" Dave feigns outrage.

"Nope! Acknowledging the historical atrocities committed by our forefathers is not treachery." Ed replies.

"Yeah, of course! So easy to acknowledge and apologize about the historical mistakes sitting here, in London, mate. If it were Iran, you would have been killed, like Reza." Dave says bitterly.

"What do you mean? Do you know who killed Reza?" Luiza asks.

"Everyone knows that, don't they? Why did Reza come here in the first place? All those years ago?"

"To study, I suppose!" Louis replies.

"Nope. He was driven out of Iran. The Khomeini government would have hanged him had he not fled the country."

"Really? How do you know all this?" I ask Dave.

"You remember, I had to re-do the experiments in his lab just before the exam in the last semester? One day I was working late in the evening. Reza was also there. That day we chatted a lot and he himself told me these stories."

"Perhaps he came to work late THAT day, too!" says Sadia in a low voice.

No one else said anything.

"But could he be killed for something that old? After all these years?" I ask.

"Well, I think it is plausible. You don't know our government." Mohammad sounds bitter.

"All governments are bad. But how did the murderer enter? No one can get into the lab without the swipe card, right?"

"Unless…" I start saying.

"Unless what?" Louis asks.

"Unless Reza himself let him in." I finish my sentence.

"That means someone he knew very well… A student or a member of faculty?" Sadia enquires.

"Blimey, Sri! You are indeed talking like a detective. Perhaps you should join MI5," Dave comments.

"Or MI6," I smile.

"I heard it was some sort of poisoning. That's why the lab is still sealed," Mohammed mentions.

"I know, the spectroscopy lab is also sealed. Don't know when I will be able to re-do that diffraction experiment." I lament.

"That's obvious, isn't it? Those two labs are adjacent with just a wall in between," Ed reminds us.

"But what kind of poison could it be? All these people in hazmat suits, with Geiger Counters in their hands…" asks Dave looking at me.

"How would I know? Am I a real detective?" I snap.

"No, you will never be a real sleuth Sri, you are so sloppy! Did you get your phone back?" asks Sadia, smiling.

"Yeah. I left it at Aunt Shukla's. The battery died so it wasn't ringing. Yesterday uncle Pavitro came to return it."

"Sri, the sloppy sleuth." Dave smiles mischievously.

"Stop pulling Sri's leg all the time. Do you know who is the real sloppy man? That's Professor Kowalski." Mike comes to my defence.

"Why? What did that old snob do now?" Ed asks.

Professor Kowalski has quite a reputation for being rather old school. He is good at condensed matter theory, for sure. But he hates modern technologies and has a habit of being dismissive towards women. All the female students hate him.

"You won't believe what he did this time. I was working in the library, and he called me for help. When I went to his desk, he sheepishly told me that he lost his mouse." Mike starts laughing.

"His mouse? What is that supposed to mean?" Dave giggles.

"Poor sod, he connected his laptop to a double monitor. Then he used the mousepad, but he couldn't find the cursor, obviously because it was on the other screen. Thus, he lost his 'mouse.'" Mike roars in laughter, and we all join in.

"Seriously, Professor Kowalski hates technology. The other day he had to give a presentation on the quantum phase transition, and he came with the transparent sheets. Not a PowerPoint presentation but transparent sheets, can you believe it, man?" Ed looks amused.

"He must have time travelled from the 1980s." Mike says, giggling.

"Yeah, he must be the original Marty McFly!" Dave comes in with his genius suggestions.

"Right, only his 'doc' couldn't find him."

Another roar of laughter at Ed's suggestion.

"Alright folks, enough of Kowalski bashing, now time to do some serious planning. Are you all going to Reza's this evening?" Luiza changes the subject.

"I can't make it, sorry! I have a tennis match." Louis says apologetically.

"Me neither. I have a night shift at the restaurant." Mohammad works part time at a Middle Eastern restaurant.

"Ok, so the rest… please chip in. We need to buy a bouquet and a card." Luiza says.

"Fuck! It's the end of the month. I already spent my entire pocket money. Have to ask dad for money again." Dave says.

"Same here," Ed comments.

"Still, we have to chip in. Can't go there empty handed. So, guys, beg, borrow, or steal." Luiza is stern.

At least they have parents to turn to. What should I do? My scholarship barely covers the expenses in this costly city. Seems no more takeaways for me this month. I will cook. That's way cheaper.

## *The Mystery of Numbers*

We meet Reza's widow, Irene Black, at their house in Islington. Nestled in a quiet, leafy street, lined with Victorian terraced houses, Reza's house features large bay windows and a front garden adorned with a roses and shrubs. They are childless, have a Labrador and a house full of books. Books are everywhere; not just in regular places like in the study or on bookshelves, but literally everywhere; The walls of the hallway are lined with bookshelves, each crammed with an eclectic mix of titles ranging from classic literature to contemporary philosophy, modern science, political theory, and cultural studies. There are books also in the kitchen, in bathrooms, in the corridor, in the conservatory.

The living room is a cozy haven, dominated by more bookshelves that reach from floor to ceiling. Comfortable, worn-in leather armchairs and a sofa are strategically placed around a low wooden coffee table, which is inevitably piled high with the professor's recent reading materials, journals, papers, and books. A large, antique Persian rug covers the floor, perhaps a nod to Reza's ancestry, and adds a touch of warmth and colour to the room. There are even stacks of books on the living room floor. A sturdy oak desk, cluttered yet orderly, sits by one of the bay windows, providing a perfect workspace that is flooded with natural light during the day. I would love to live in a house like this! This is my dream house — not a house like Aunt Shukla's — tidy, clean, immaculate but so very impersonal and soulless.

"How long have you known each other?" Luiza asks Irene.

"For about thirty years now. We have been married for twenty-seven years. I knew him for a couple of years before that," reminisces Irene.

"Are you staying alone in this house now?" I ask her.

"Well, from now on I have to stay alone, I suppose! But right now, my brother and his wife are staying with me." Irene replies in a soft voice.

"Any relatives of Reza…?" I enquire.

"No. His parents are long dead. He got the news but could not even bid them farewell. I heard that in her last days, his mother always used to stare at the door, hoping for him to return…"

How terrible! I could not help thinking. I am also a foreigner, staying in a faraway land. But there is no comparison with Reza. Thirty-two bloody years! Never been able to go back to see his parents or family. The kind of price some people pay for their principles!

"When you spoke to him last, I mean that night, did he seem alright to you?" Ed asks hesitantly.
"Yeah. He just called and said everyone has already left, he was alone in the lab, and he would stay to finish his paper," Irene comments.
"Was he very busy? I mean staying back at lab the whole night, did he use to do that often?" I ask the question which had been bothering me for some time now.
"Well, he didn't of course do that on a regular basis, but he did it sometimes, especially if any submission deadline for a big journal was approaching," Irene replies.
"
"

"Do you know, by any chance, what was he working on? Who were his collaborators?" I keep pressing. Luiza gives me an angry look. She doesn't like my interrogation of the aggrieved widow. But I ignore her, and Irene replies, "Well, I can't say for sure I am not a scientist, you see! He did not discuss work with me. But he was busy… always on his laptop, for the last few days. And he did talk about a submission deadline. I naturally thought he meant a new paper. Maybe that's why he was working late in the lab that day."

Interesting! It would be nice to know what Reza was up to, for example, but I cannot pester Irene any more on this right now. It would be inappropriate and Luiza would kill me.

"Have they told you the cause of death yet?" Sahil asks.
"No. They are still investigating, it seems. Anyway, it doesn't matter anymore, does it?" replies Irene in her low, soft voice, keeping her gaze fixed on the carpet.

She is right, nothing will bring Reza back now. But why should an autopsy report take this long, I keep thinking as I enter Suparna's terraced house. I rang her to confirm a while ago. But my heart just skipped a beat as my eyes fell on the person opening the door.

It was Neil!

Shit! What is this irritating pain-in-the-arse doing here?

"Ms. Marple! What brings you here? Are you following me?" asks the arrogant prick.
"I came to visit Suparna." I reply coldly.
"I see. Come in then. Sups, your guest is here." Neil stands aside to let me in.

Suparna seems genuinely pleased to see me. This is also a lovely house with décor that is a harmonious blend of the old and the new, reflecting the occupants' love for tradition and innovation. The floors are wooden, creaking gently with age, and the high ceilings and large windows create a sense of space and light. Artifacts collected from travels abroad – a Greek vase, an African mask, a Chinese scroll – add a worldly touch to the interiors. This house is also full of books which I take time to browse through. We chat for a while and then she insists that I must stay for dinner. I try to decline but am firmly turned down.

I meet Neil's dad Dr. Aniket Basu, the cardiologist, at the dinner table. He is still quite handsome and very fit.

"Do you guys know each other?" Suparna asks me and Neil, as she serves the salad.
"Yeah, I met her at her Uni, when I went there to investigate the murder of Professor Tavacol," Neil replies.
"So, it definitely is a murder, then?" I ask.

"Well, at least it was not a cardiac arrest or stroke or similar medical condition. At least that's what the autopsy report says," he replies.

"What does the Geiger Counter say?" I ask as I take a spoonful of rice onto my plate.

"Nothing. The radiation level is not too high."

"So why don't you open our labs then? It's bloody inconvenient, you see…"

"We can't do that before we make sure that there is no trace of any other fatal substance present there."

"What fatal substance?" I ask.

"Don't know, some nerve agent perhaps… like Novichok," Neil replies.

"Novichok? Isn't that illegal?" asked Aniket.

"It is, dad, as per the UN regulation. But many rogue nations still use it," Neil replies.

"Prof. Tavacol was of Iranian origin, right?" Suparna enquires.

"Yes, he was. But he left Iran thirty-two years ago. Never went back there," Neil replies.

"Khomeini government ordered Reza to be hanged," I tell them as I take some chicken curry onto my plate.

"How do you know all this?" asks Neil, squinting.

"From his widow, Irene. We met her today, to offer our condolences."

"To offer condolences or to sleuth?" asks Neil dryly as he takes some chicken.

"Jesus! Why would I sleuth? Am I a detective, like you? Reza was our professor… it's only polite to meet his widow after such an incident." I'm feeling truly annoyed.

Both Aniket and Suparna have become a bit startled at the tone of our conversation.

"Why sleuthing, son? Sri is a student of that deceased professor, so obviously…" Aniket wants to calm things down.

"There are reasons why I am saying this, dad. We have information that a private detective is also trying to probe into this case. Everyone wants to be Sherlock Holmes!" says Neil, with a wry smile.

"Or Byomkesh Bakshi, right Sri?" Aniket mentions the famous fictional detective of Bengali literature. He wants to divert the discussion to defuse the tension, I suppose.

"Do you read Bakshi, Sri? Do you like crime thrillers?" Dr. Basu continues.

"Yes, I read Bakshi and I like it. But I don't like the others. Especially the most famous one." I reply.

"Really? Why?"

"Because that one is so male chauvinistic. If you read it, you would feel that the world is totally devoid of women. They just don't exist. Forget about the main characters, there is not even a minor female character in there. Basically, I can't relate to it at all."

"Interesting! It used to be quite popular back in our days!" Aniket comments.

"It is still quite popular. But not so much among the younger generations, anymore. It is a bit dated, in my opinion."

"You are absolutely right, Sri. I think so, too," agrees Suparna.

"But Bakshi is even older," Aniket correctly points out.

"True. But in Bakshi, or for that matter even in Sherlock Holmes, the society of that era is truthfully depicted. I can take that. But I can't swallow it when they artificially remove all female references from fairly recent seventies or eighties society," I explain.

"Excuse me! Please don't forget that I am also sitting here. These discussions about the Bengali literature are going above my head," says Neil.

"Why Neil? I tried so much to teach you the language when you were little..." Dr. Basu sounds a little disappointed.

"Don't lie, dad! When did you teach me? Did you ever have time for it? And mum isn't Bengali. Actually, Sups taught me a few words after she came in... like *paji*," Neil quickly glances over at me.

"Hmm. Well, perhaps it is my fault, then," Dr. Basu admits.

"Neil, don't try to guilt trip your dad. You could have learnt it if you wanted to. In fact, Linda knows more Bengali than you. She always greets me in Bengali whenever I call her." Suparna says.

"Who is Linda?" I ask.

"Neil's mum," Suparna explains.

"Mum learnt it to impress dad." Neil smiles.

"You can also learn it to impress your dad!" Suparna smiles back.

"Did you speak to Linda recently?" Aniket asks Suparna.

"No. Why?"

"I wanted to check how Kevin doing after his bypass surgery," Aniket says.

"Kevin is a very difficult patient to care for, dad. Never gives up on bacon and burgers," Neil informs Aniket with a smile and then looks at me to explain, "Kevin is my stepdad. He and Mum live in Scotland."

They keep talking and I start thinking of my friend Avro in Kolkata. His parents got divorced when he was in year nine. Even now they cannot stand one another. They always pounce on each other and create a scene if they bump into one another accidentally at any mutual gathering. Avro used to be a good student, a happy boy. But all this mudslinging, screaming and custody battles had a terrible impact on him. He withdrew from his friends, his grades started falling and he dropped out of school after serious drug abuse. But Neil's parents seemed to have dealt with it in a much more civilized and friendly way.

"How will you get back, Sri?" asks Suparna after the dinner.

"I'll take the underground."

"But that's a long way, why don't you go with Neil? He has got a car and can drop you off."

"No! No need for that. I'll take the public transport, no worries," I say quickly.

"I think Sri is angry with Neil because of his comments about sleuthing and all, you know!" Aniket is a clever man, he guesses it right.

"It's not my fault if someone can't take a joke!" comments Neil, as he looks at me through the corner of his eyes.

"Look Neil, everyone will be angry with you if you keep talking like this," Suparna scolds him and then tells me, "Don't be angry, Sri. Go with Neil, he often pretends to be obnoxious, but is actually a good boy. It will be so much simpler for you."

\*\*\*

"Are you still cross with me?" asks Neil as he starts his car.

"No."

"That means you are. Those monosyllabic answers mean exactly that," he smirks.

"Your parents are so nice. How come you are such a prick?"

"Where did you see my parents? You only saw my dad. Sups is not my mum."

"Sorry, I thought you liked her."

"I do. She is a nice person. But she is not my mum. I like my stepdad Kevin too. But he is not my dad either."

I remain quiet. I'm not too familiar with such family dynamics. My background is different. Neil keeps driving through busy London streets.

"I know it may look strange to you," Neil says again, almost reading my mind. "We have our ancestral home in Kolkata. I have been there a few times. My aunts used to ask me if my stepdad beats me, or my stepmum starves me," says Neil with a wry smile.

"Sorry. But I don't think that way at all."

"I know. You are from a different generation. Educated, well-travelled," Neil comments in a matter-of-fact way.

"How did you meet Sups?" he asks again.

"She is a friend of my aunt. Some Bengali connection, I suppose," I reply.

"I see! Do you live with your aunt here?"

"No! My aunt lives in Wimbledon, and I live in Canning Town. Where do you live?"

"In Notting Hill."

"Alone? Or with your girlfriend?"

"I don't have a girlfriend. Otherwise, I would not have asked you out. I am not a real James Bond, you see!"

"You didn't ask me out, you were just pulling my leg."

"Are you sure?"

"What is that supposed to mean?"

"Never mind! I don't have a girlfriend because we have to be mindful who we mingle with. Moreover, I have serious commitment phobia." Neil smiles.

"Hmm… I know, it is rather common in children from broken families."

"Jesus! My family is not broken. It's blended."

"Sorry! Actually, I come from a very different background," I confess. "My parents have been together for thirty years. Have been married for almost twenty-six years now," I try to explain.

"Hmm. Do you expect the same for yourself? One relationship for life?"

"Never thought of it!" I give a truthful answer.

"If you don't mind my asking, did you ever have a boyfriend?"

"No."

"How old are you?"

"Twenty-three."

"Blimey! A twenty-three-year-old virgin! How extraordinary."

"Did I tell you whether I am a virgin or not? Stop the car, I will get out and take the tube from here," I reply angrily. This man is really getting on my nerves. All these discussions are totally pointless and this kind of belittling me is totally uncalled for. Suparna was wrong; he does not *pretend* to be obnoxious; he *is* obnoxious.

"Look, you don't have to say it categorically. You do not exactly give the one-night-stand kind of a vibe. Never had a boyfriend either. So, I am just connecting the dots here!" Neil isn't done with his outrageous comments on my personal life.

"I see! Did you connect any dots for Reza's murder yet?"

"Now that you ask, I did connect a few dots there, actually! But I can't give you any details yet, I'm afraid."

"Why not? You didn't detect any radiation in your Geiger. Doesn't that make this case simpler?"

"Does it, Ms. Marple? At least with radiation we could have been certain about the murder weapon. Now we have nothing. There is no wound on the body, no evidence of poisoning. This is not at all a simple case," says Neil in a solemn voice.

"So, the motive and the means, both are unclear!" I comment.

"Why? You just said the means could be political persecution. That's the result of your investigation today, isn't it?" This man has enormous ability to harp on the same thing.

"I told you I did not go there to investigate."

As I shake my head to emphasize my words, my glasses slip off my nose and fall on the floor of the car. I try to retrieve them but do not succeed. They are stuck under the seat.

"You can't get it out like that. Let me pull over and then you can slide your seat back to retrieve them," suggests Neil as he steers the car towards a bus stop.

Bending down, I am still trying to retrieve my specs from under the seat when the car stops. Neil presses the brake exactly when I was trying to get up again and I bump my head hard against the dashboard.

"Ouch!" I let out a cry.

"You are the sloppiest sleuth I have ever seen, Ms. Marple!" comments Neil as he fishes my specs out from under the floor beneath my seat and hands them over to me.

"Why do you keep calling me a sleuth? I am a student," I tell him as I put the glasses back on.

"You can do anything for a living, Ms. Marple, it doesn't matter. But you're a sleuth in spirit." Neil smiles as he starts the car again.

"Did you get the autopsy report yet?" I ask.

"Yes. But it is confidential. We can't make it public yet," Neil replies.

"I see. That's why you did not tell it to Irene either. Why can't you? People needs closure, you know?"

"Yes, I know. But we can't divulge sensitive information halfway through an investigation."

"Well, you can tell me. Maybe I can help!"

There! I finally said it.

"Hmm ... won't that be risky?"

"How?"

"Who knows, you could be an accomplice to the murderer. Quite plausible. Especially the way you are following me. When you could not get hold of my number, you tracked my stepmum down to reach to me."

"God! For your information, I did not ask to come here. It was Suparna who insisted. How would I know that you would be here too?"

"Really? Didn't you know that?"

"No. And you can easily verify that I am actually a student at Queen Mary."

"So what? Spies are often given alternate identities. We do it, too. You could very well moonlight as a North Korean spy. Who knows!"

"Jesus! Why would I spy for North Korea? Didn't I tell you that I am from India?"

"You could be lying. Maybe you are actually from North Korea. Again, plausible. You actually have a flattish nose… that's why the glasses slipped off, you see!"

"This is exactly why you don't have a girlfriend! You are unimaginably rude!"

"Hmm. So, you don't moonlight as a North Korean spy, then?"

"No. I sleep at night. You can verify that with my flatmate, Matt."

"Do you have a flatmate named Matt? Perhaps both of you are spies then."

"You can't go on accusing everyone like this, without a shred of evidence. Matt is a perfect gentleman. Polite, handsome, friendly…"

"Are you sleeping with him?"

"Excuse me! Why are you so interested in my sex life?"

"You mean in your non-existent sex life?"

"Unbelievable! And what about you? You don't have any girlfriend either, right? Thanks to your charming personality, of course!"

"I have a lot more experience in life than you, Sri!" says Neil, as he sips an energy drink. Then he puts the can back into its holder and continues, "Damage in the central nervous system, bone marrow and GI track."

"Postmortem report?" I ask.

"Yes."

"But these are very broad symptoms. Could be many things…"

"Yes. Could be many things. My boss Daniel thinks it is Thallium poisoning."

"Thallium? Isn't that a bit old school?"

"Yep! Daniel is from the ancient times. But what can I do, he is the boss!" Neil says bitterly.

"Also, does Thallium poisoning damage the bone marrow?"

"No, it does not. You see, it is not easy being a junior detective. All these old farts are sitting above. They would neither do anything themselves nor would they allow others to do any meaningful work."

"Hmm. I see! So, that is why you are seeking help from a sloppy sleuth!"

"Look missy, I didn't seek help from you! You are the one who was poking her nose!"

"It is difficult to poke your nose when you have a flattish one! You said the Geiger count was normal, right?"

"Yep. No gamma ray spike detected."

"Interesting! Didn't you get any other evidence from the victim? I mean any fingerprints or anything like that?"

"Not really. No finger or footprint. No hair or body fluid from anyone other than Reza. It feels like he was alone there at the time of his death."

"That's weird, isn't it? The murderer must have been there, right?"

"Perhaps the murderer was very careful."

"Still, there's bound to be something. Did you check the card reader at the door?"

"Yes, we did. Martha left at around five that day. There are plenty of witnesses who saw her leaving. Then Reza entered the lab at around seven. No one else swiped in their card after that."

"And when exactly did he die?"

"Coroner says between one and three in the morning. Reza called his wife at around ten to inform her that he may have to stay back to finish some work."

"Did he used to do that often?"

"Not too often. But sometimes, yes."

"So, it must have been Reza himself who let the murderer in, right?"

"Good detection Ms. Marple. We suspected that, too. But there was no one that night at the department. The last person to leave the department building was a PhD student Antonio. He was working late to complete his thesis. He left at 9:30 pm. No one came in or went out between then and 7:25 am next morning when Martha came and discovered the body. We checked all door lock logs, checked all CCTV footage. So, who did Reza let in?"

"Good question."

We drive in silence for a while, then a thought comes to my mind. "Neil, I was thinking, sometimes the victim writes something before they die. Like the name of the attacker or something like that. Did Reza do anything like that?"

Neil remains silent for a while. Perhaps, he finds my suggestion amateurish; he would probably mock me for reading too many detective novels and behaving like one. We have almost reached my apartment. He parks the car in front of our building and says, "Well, now I'm going to do something which I may regret in the future; but, let me do it nevertheless…"

Suddenly, I become apprehensive. What is he planning to do? Kiss me? A romantic overture?

Thankfully, he does nothing like that, but pulls his phone out of his pocket.

"I'm not supposed to show it to you. But no one in our department has got any clue. So please have a look." He shows me a picture in his phone.

It was a number. 210-138. Written on a piece of white paper.

"This is what Reza scribbled that day on a piece of paper before he died."

"What does it mean? A phone number?"

"Just six digits?"

"Maybe he passed out before finishing the rest."

"Plausible, But I think it is something else."

"What?"

"I don't know, Ms. Marple. That's why I showed it to you. Think. Keep thinking about it whilst checking your handsome flatmate out. And let me know if you can come up with anything. My number is zero-seven-three…"

Alpha Beta Gamma

## *In the Name of Honor*

Today I have a morning class at eight, but after that I have a long break, which I decide to use to complete the solid-state assignments. So I go to the library, sit in my usual corner, spread my textbooks, notes, and laptop across the wooden table, creating a small fortress of knowledge around me. It is a nice and sunny, crisp autumn day outside, but I am determined to stay focused. I work straight for hours, only taking a couple of breaks to stretch my legs and refill my coffee. I even keep my phone on silent. I glance at the clock and realise that I have been working steadily for three hours. My stomach grumbles, reminding me that lunch is overdue. I decide to wrap up and head for the cafeteria.

I really must re-do the diffraction pattern experiment now. The labs opened again yesterday. Except for Reza's condensed matter lab, which is still sealed. But all labs have now built up a huge backlog because all students from all years are rushing to finish their pending experiments. I finally manage to get a slot at four PM at the spectroscopy lab after nagging the person in charge, Helena Swift, for hours. But now I have got another problem. Ed is my partner in this experiment, but there is no trace of him all morning. He is not even picking up his bloody phone. Sadia is not coming to college either. I have no idea what's going on, I just hope they didn't elope!

As I am going towards the department after buying an apple and a yoghurt from the cafeteria, I hear someone calling me: "Sri!"

"Ed! Where have you been? We must be in the lab soon. I literally begged Helena to get this slot. Come now."

"One moment, Sri. Please come with me…"

"Where? What is going on Ed?"

Without replying, Ed grabs my hand and drags me towards the back lawn. Now I notice that he looks rather scruffy and dishevelled. We come to the west corner. This part of the campus is not very well maintained, the overgrown of grass and weeds and the non-functioning fountain clearly prove that. There is a wooden bench under a huge oak tree. Not many people come here, except for couples looking for some privacy.

"What's the matter, Ed?" I ask again.

Without replying he points his finger towards the bench. Sadia is sitting there. But what on earth has happened to her? Her hair is all messy, the face swollen, she has got a black eye and a big cut above her upper lip.

"What happened, Sadia? Who did this to you?"

She does not say anything, but Ed spoke.

"Her family did this."

"What! Why?"

"Her uncle saw us the other day, we were coming out of the movie theatre. They beat her and locked her up in her room, confiscated her phone. She was forbidden to come to college, too. Apparently, higher education for girls brings such insolence and shame to the family. Her cousin will soon fly from Pakistan, and she will be forced to marry him."

"What do you mean forced to marry him? Is this a civilized country or not? Don't you have law and order here?" I blurt out angrily.

"Did you go to the police?" I ask.

"I told her to. But she is not willing to go." Ed replies.

"My younger sister secretly opened the door to let me out. If I go to the police, they will kill her." Sadia finally speaks.

I am really at my wit's end. Which era is this? Feels like the mediaeval times. I have heard about similar stories, it used to happen during our parents'…no, no, our grandparents' time. But this is 2023 for God's sake and this is London!

"Where will you stay now, Sadia? With Ed?" I ask again.

"I asked her… but she says no." Ed replied.

"They have extracted all the details about Ed from me. They will go his place first." Sadia says.

"Will you stay with me then?" I offer.

"No. They may go to your place, too. They got the details of all my friends."

"What a pickle! What will you do then? Sadia, listen, you need to contact the police."

"No! Farida… my sister… they will kill her."

Sadia looks scared and on the verge of crying.

"They will not actually kill her, will they? She is their own daughter…" I try to reason with her.

"You have no idea, Sri! Do you think all families are like yours? Liberal, educated? Haven't you ever heard of honour killing? Do you know how many falls victim to honour killings every year in the UK?"

"Then there is all the more reason to call the police," I say in a firm tone.

"What for? The police will call them or will send an officer to question. My parents, will somehow hoodwink the officer and as soon as he leaves, they will turn on Farida."

Sadia seems not very hopeful about police help.

"Umm, then I suppose the police need to handle this delicately, keeping your and Farida's safety in mind. We need a sympathetic officer."

"Where would we get such a made to order sympathetic officer?" asks Ed bitterly.

"Let me try."

I take my phone out and dial Neil's number.

"Yes, Ms. Marple! Did you crack the number puzzle already?"

Neil asks directly after picking up the phone.

"Neil… I mean Mr. Basu…"

"Neil is fine."

"Actually, I need your help. My friend, Sadia …"

I tell him everything over the phone and Neil Basu arrives at the campus within twenty minutes.

"Thanks, Neil. Actually, we…"

Neil gestures me to stop and asks Sadia directly, "Your sister, Farida, how old is she?"

"Nineteen," Sadia replies.

"Good. Then she is not a minor. We can bring her out."

"Bring her out? Where to? She does not have any money, she has her college…" Sadia sounds alarmed.

"To the Hounslow Asian Sisters charity. For now. They run a safehouse. Mainly for such victims of honour killings or domestic abuse. I have already spoken to them. Almost ninety five percent of their inhabitants are from the subcontinent. Thanks to our wonderful tradition, of course," says Neil sarcastically.

"Not everyone in the subcontinent is the same—" I start, but Neil cuts me off mid-sentence.

"I know that! Don't forget that I partially belong to that heritage, too. In no culture is everyone the same, there are always variations. But it is no good to remain blind about one's shortcomings either. How would you feel if everyone here praised the British colonies?"

I did not have any answer to that. Neil spoke to Sadia again. "You have to lodge a formal complaint. And a police doctor will examine you."

"But…"

"Don't worry. I will arrange everything. There are already two plain clothed officers posted outside your home. You will come with me now, submit the report and then we shall take your sister to Hounslow Sisters."

"What about me?"

"Oh… I thought you would stay with your boyfriend. Hounslow Sisters only have one place available now."

"Of course, she can stay with me if she wants… I mean my parents will be OK with that, I think," Ed says hesitantly.

"Oh, I see. you live with your parents! Yes, of course, you are all students, kids!" says Mr. Basu patronizingly. I again think about what Suparna said about him; she said that Neil pretends to be obnoxious, but I think he doesn't need much pretending, it comes naturally to him.

"I do not live with my parents. Sadia will stay with me." I volunteer.

"That's good. But what about your roommate?" Neil asks.

"Matt is my flatmate; we do not share a room. He will be fine, I am sure about that. He is so nice and sweet and understanding and…"

"Yeah, yeah, the sun rises from Matt the great's behind, we all know that. Now let us go. Shall we?"

Neil takes the three of us to his car. First, we go to the police station where Sadia lodges a formal complaint. By then, two police officers have brought Farida there. After the emotional reunion of the two sisters, we all head for Hounslow. We help them complete the formalities at the charity's office and take Farida to her new accommodation. It's pretty basic, and she has to share her room with another girl, but at least it was clean and tidy, and most importantly, safe. Finally, when Sadia and I enter our apartment, it's eight thirty in the evening.

Matt is at home. I send Sadia to my room and briefly explain the situation to him. As expected, he is very supportive and says Sadia can stay here as long as she wants. He even offers to convert his study into a makeshift guest room for her, in case my room feels too crowded.

I let Sadia change and settle down a bit. She has had a very long and stressful day. Then we gave dinner together. Matt again cooks, a brilliant mushroom risotto with parmesan cheese for all of us. After diner, the three of us are sitting in front of the telly, watching a rerun of Friends in the living room. Nothing lifts the mood up better than a few episodes of Friends. I can see that Sadia is slowly coming back to her normal self again.

Suddenly, the doorbell rings. We get a little startled. Who could it be, so late in the evening? I am sitting closest to the door, so I get up to open it.

But suddenly, Matt shoots up from the sofa like a bullet and stops me. Then he rushes to the door himself, has a quick look through the eyehole and runs back to us. He pulls Sadia by her hand and starts dragging her towards his room. Both Sadia and I are gobsmacked.

"They are here. Sadia's family, I think. They are armed. We have to act smart. Sri, you go and open the door. Tell them Sadia is not here and I am in my room with my girlfriend. Clear?"

Matt whispers as he drags a frozen Sadia to his room. I nod sheepishly.

"Now go and open the door." Matt says, standing at the door of his room.

"What if we don't? Can't we just dial 999?"

"They will break the door before the police arrives. Do as I say. Keep a cool head."

Matt takes Sadia into his room and closes the door.

\*\*\*

The banging grows louder and more urgent, and I fear they might break the door open. Reluctantly, I open the door, and they immediately shove me aside and storm in. There are three men, one armed with a knife, another wielding an iron chain, and the third with his hands ominously tucked in his pockets. They look around and ask, "Where is that bitch?"

"Who?"

"Don't play innocent, OK? Sadia, where did you hide her?"

They speak in Urdu.

"Who are you? Why are you looking for her?"

I gather courage to ask the questions.

"Don't try to act smart! Not too many questions, understand? Just answer what we ask."

"She is not here." I lie.

"Where is your room? Show us."

I show them to my room. The search is thorough. They comb through every inch of my en-suite bathroom, open the closet, peer under the bed, and rifle through all my personal belongings. Satisfied they had left no stone unturned, they leave my room and move on to Matt's study. I can hear them repeating the same methodical process. Next, they spread out, systematically sweeping through the rest of the flat. They ransack the kitchen, inspect the main bathroom, check the storeroom, and even scrutinize the balcony.

I stand silently in the living room, watching their every move. My heart pounds, but I keep my expression neutral, hoping they won't notice my unease.

Finally, they come back to me and point towards the closed door of Matt's room.

"Whose room is that?"

"My flatmate, Matt."

As they turn towards that room I implore to them, "Please… don't go there. He is in there… with his girlfriend."

But they ignore me and started banging on the closed door.

Soon Matt comes and opens the door. He is only in his boxer shorts, his hair ruffled up.

"Yes? Who are these guys, Sri?" he asks, looking at me.

Before I can say anything, they shove him aside and go inside the room. I follow them. The light is very dim inside, the bed messy. The dim light in the room casts long shadows, giving the room an eerie atmosphere.

There, lying with her back towards us, was a girl. The soft glow from a nearby lamp highlighted her golden blonde hair, cascading over the pillow in delicate waves. Her skin, partially covered by the duvet, was smooth and fair. But what caught my attention immediately was the intricate snake tattoo that coils along her bare back, its scales detailed with precision, the head resting just below her shoulder blade.

Sadia's hair is not blonde. She does not have any tattoo on her back.

"Do you mind, guys? My girlfriend is getting uncomfortable," Matt says.

"Let's go guys. Leave this bitch and her lover alone. Seems we have disturbed them in the middle of their business." They wink and laugh distastefully, but I breathe a sigh of relief when they all went back to the living room.

They start interrogating me again in the living room.
"Are you from India?"
"Yes."
"What are you doing here? Alone?"
"I came to study."
"Why? Isn't there any Uni in India? Bloody excuses! Do you also sleep with that whitey boy? You horny bitch?"
I can feel my cheeks getting flustered, my head spinning from this barrage of verbal abuse. But I keep my cool. There is no point getting into an argument with this bunch of armed thugs.

"Do you really not know where Sadia is?" another man asks.
"No. She has other friends, too." I reply.
"We know. We have been to that boyfriend's place too. She is not there either."
"Perhaps she is getting help from the police." I want to scare them away.

"What police? We are doing it for the first time, OK? We have done this before, many times. You modern girls, you bring shame to your families. You have this habit of going out with these Brit boys…you leave us with no choice," the man with the chain says angrily. Victim shaming at its best.

"But this time the police are a bit more active than usual. Seems like someone higher up is pulling the strings," says the man with the knife.

"Yeah. Tell us, who is your sympathizer in the police force? Normally they ignore our internal affairs. We have brought many girls from our community to their senses before, police never bothered us. Now where did you get this sympathizer of yours?" the man with the iron chain asks again.

"P-Police… I mean…"

"Yes, Police. Tell me who is helping you. What's is his name…?"

I can feel the cold knife blade against the skin of my neck.

"The name is Neil. Neil Basu. MI6, Anti-Terror branch."

The male voice comes from the open door. We never locked it after these thugs barged in. Now Neil has entered through the open door, holding a gun in his hand. There are two other armed Met police officers behind him. The intruders have raised their hands above their heads.

I felt a great sense of relief as I saw Neil. The tension that had been building up seemed to dissipate slightly.

"Everyone, stay calm," Neil commands, his voice steady and authoritative. The intruders comply, their expressions a mix of fear and resignation.

The Met officers swiftly move in, disarming the thugs and securing the room. Neil approaches me, his eyes scanning for any signs of injury.

"Are you okay?" he asks.

I nod, my voice barely a whisper, "Yes, just shaken up."

After the Met officers handcuff the thugs and take them away with them, I speak to him, "Thanks Neil. But how did you …?"

"Ed called me. They had also been to his place. I thought maybe they would come here now, so I came to check. Seems my hunch was correct. Is Sadia fine?"

"Yes, Matt helped us a lot. Wait, let me call them."

We knock his door again and Matt again comes to open it. But this time he has a gun in his hand. Surprised to see Neil, he looks at me.

"It's alright Matt. Neil is in MI6," I assure him.

"Oh! I thought perhaps those guys had suspected something and came back again. That's why this," he indicated the gun in his hand.

"It is licensed, I hope?" Neil asks.

"Sure. I can show you if you want," Matt says.

"No, that's fine. Sadia?"

"She is there. Sadia, all clear."

Sadia gets up and removes her golden blonde wig.

"This is my date Sandra's wig," Matt explains.

"Clever!" Neil praises.

"And the tattoo?" I ask.

"Oh, those are children's stuff, temporary tattoos. Stays for a couple of days and then washes off. I have loads of them, see!" Matt opens his bedside drawer.

"Impressive!" Neil says again.

"Alright, Matt, thanks a lot. You and Sadia can put your clothes on now. I have to leave."

Both Matt and Sadia look a bit embarrassed by Neil's comment. Typical of Neil, enjoying putting people in an uncomfortable position.

"Bye, Sri. I hope there won't be any more trouble now. But if there is, don't hesitate to call me," says Neil as we near the door.

"And, if I may say so, good choice!" he smiles.

"What?" I say, surprised.

"Matt, I mean. Clever, resourceful. And the physique…even a straight guy like me was finding it hard not to look!"

"What choice? He is my flatmate, that's all!"

"No! That's not all! You fancy him."

"No. That's absolutely—"

## Alpha Beta Gamma

"You are a terrible liar, Sri! Goodnight."

***

Neil goes home, Matt goes to his room, Sadia is sleeping on the couch. As I put my head on the pillow and switch the lights off in my room, the picture of Matt in boxer shorts flashes before my closed eyes. The darkness of my room seems to grow heavier as I replay the image of Matt and Sadia in my mind. I squeeze my eyes shut tighter, willing the thoughts to vanish, but they only grow clearer.
"Stop it," I mutter to myself, gripping the pillow. Sadia has been through enough already. She doesn't deserve my jealousy on top of everything else. Matt was just being a good friend, helping her when she needed it most.

But again, I think of the messy bed, with Sadia in there, with her bare back. Suddenly, I feel a sharp pang of jealousy.

No! This is terrible, I am a terrible person. Poor Sadia, those thugs would have killed her otherwise. Matt just helped her… but her smooth, buttery skin… so sensuous with that snake tattoo. Matt must have helped her with that tattoo… the golden locks flowing over the tattoo…

Suddenly I sit upright and switch the bedside lamp on. That golden wig, where did it come from? Who is Sandra? I know who came here in last few weeks. Martha, Kate, Kathy… no, no, Casey, Gina, Simran, Becky… and that girl with black hair… forgot her name but it was not Sandra. None of them wore any golden wig like that. So? What does it mean? And those temporary tattoos, why does he keep them? He is not a child!

Wig, tattoo… means for disguise? Why does he need this stuff? And he is so quick… the way he jumped up and stopped me from opening the door, so fast… like a panther… or a trained spy. And that loaded gun, why does he need that?

God, I don't even know what he does for a living. He owns an agency, but what agency? I assumed it to be a travel agency. What if it is not? What is his line of work?

Work! What about my work?
Shit! Shit! Shit! Holy crap!

I didn't even go to the spectroscopy lab in the afternoon today. I pleaded so hard to get the four PM slot today, but now I blew it. My career will be sacrificed at the altar of Ed and Sadia's relationship. And these two handsome hunks… Neil and Matt… none of them are simple, straightforward blokes. They both have tons of cards up their sleeves which they are not showing to me. Why on earth did I get into this?

My diffraction data… what will I do? Helena will kill me!

\*\*\*

It is 7:40 am when I get down from the train at Mile End. I came early to catch Helena in the first hour. Convincing her to give me another slot is crucial; my experiment depends on it. Sadia was still sleeping when I left. After all the chaos last night, I didn't have the heart to wake her. She needed the rest and could come in later.

Helena usually arrived by eight-thirty. I hoped she would understand that I had an emergency. If needed, I could ask Neil to vouch for me. He knew how much this meant. I took a deep breath and prepared myself for the conversation.

I saw Reza's lab still closed as I was passing by the corridor on the ground floor. Prof Kowalski will step in for Reza and will help us in the condensed matter lab when it opens. Next is the spectroscopy lab. The door is open. Is Helena already in?

But I can't see anyone inside.

"Helena!" No one answers.

I go towards the door leading to the dark room inside. The spectroscopy lab is pitch dark, as it should be. It took me a while to get used to the darkness there. There isn't anyone here either. The room is empty. The Frenal bi-prism apparatus is on the left-hand side.

On the right-hand side there are three spectrometers on the table. I go straight in, towards the far wall. The diffraction setup is there…

Oh my! What is that? In front of the diffraction setup, there is somebody lying on her tummy.

I rush towards her. Helena! It's Helena.

I take her hand to check the pulse, but there is no need. She is stone cold. And hard. Rigor mortis set in a while back. She must have been dead for hours.

Another professor is dead. Within ten days. What should I do now? What am I supposed to do? I dial Neil almost on autopilot.

"Yes, Ms. Marple…?" Neil sounds sleepy.
"Neil… Neil… p-please come over…"

"What happened, Sri?" Neil is fully alert. "Where are you calling from? Is Sadia alright? Matt?" he keeps asking.

"They are fine, Neil. I'm in college… And… here… Professor Helena Swift… she is dead, Neil…"

"What? Where?"

"In the spectroscopy lab."

"Isn't that one just adjacent to Reza's?"

"Yes…"

"Get out, Sri. Get out immediately. Don't touch the body. Don't touch anything there. I'm coming…"

"But I checked her pulse…"

"Shit! Anyway. Get out and don't touch anything else. Tell others not to enter before the police come. I'm on my way."

"What are you thinking Neil? Radiation? Am I contaminated?" I almost whisper.

"I don't know, Sri! We have to check that. But don't worry…"

I can hear the street noise. He is already out.

"I'm not worried." I whisper as I disconnected the call.

\*\*\*

Sitting at the restaurant just outside our college, I order a pizza. The whole morning is a blur. It's deja-vu with Police, ambulance, hazmat suits, Geiger Counters. All classes are dismissed once again.

This time I am interrogated extensively because I discovered the body first. Neil was there the whole time though. They also did check me up for the radiation exposure. The result was negative. Such a relief. Still Neil asked me to change my clothes, just to be on the safe side.

Neil looks relived after the doctors give me the clean chit. But I am not. I feel shattered. What the hell is going on? One murder after another, in a physics department. It doesn't make any sense. All students and faculties are worried and puzzled at the same time. God knows how long the labs will be closed this time. I will never be able to finish my diffraction experiment, it seems. It is jinxed.

It is two in the afternoon now. The restaurant is rather empty. Just as I got the pizza on my table, Ed came and sat opposite to me. I remembered that I had not seen him since the morning.

"Hi, Sri! You alright?"
"Yeah… I'm fine."
"Honestly, what the fuck is happening here?"
"No idea!"
"Did you find the body?"
"Yes."
"But Helena almost never worked very late at night in the lab…"

"I don't think she intended to spend the night in the lab. Perhaps she came in the evening. Most likely to check our setup. We were supposed to do the diffraction experiment yesterday, remember? She must have gone back soon, unless she was killed before that."

"Her family? Didn't they call when she didn't return home at night?"

"Helena used to live alone. Her mum called her from Devon at around 9 PM. No one picked up the phone. She thought maybe Helena was busy. Thought of calling her again in the morning."

"But why? Why all these killings? One after another…?"

"I really don't know, Ed. But why didn't you come in the morning?"

"How could I? Last night Sadia's relatives came and threatened us. Even broke some furniture in our house… complete thugs. My parents are very upset. This morning we went to the police station, lodged a complaint, and got a restraining order. What a mess! If I knew it would be such a big problem…"

Ed doesn't finish his sentence.

"What? If you knew it would be such a big issue, would you not go out with Sadia? Would you dump her?"

"Be reasonable, Sri! We have just started going out, it has not even been two months yet, we have not even slept together. And already it's such a big nuisance… what the hell!"

"Sadia left her family because of you!" I reminded him sternly.

"No Sri! Sadia did not leave because of me. She left because she was getting abused there. I want to save her from that, sure, as a friend. But…"

"But what?"

"Come on, Sri! We are just twenty-three. We are still students. We have our exams, careers to sort out. What can I do? Marry her? Will you get married now?"

"Have you lost your marbles? Who gets married at twenty-three?"

"Then? Why should I…?"

"What will happen to Sadia then? Where will she stay? And her sister?"

"I really don't know, Sri. You can blame me if you want. But think about it for a moment. We just started going out, like any two normal people in the Uni. If everything went smoothly, then, perhaps sometime in the future, we could have settled down and had a family and all that. Or maybe not, who knows? It's too early to say, anyway. But now… everything started happening so fast and so dramatically… I'm not ready. And to be honest, I don't think Sadia is ready either!"

I don't know what Sadia is doing now. She didn't come to the college today. I am really getting worried about her. What will happen to her? Where will she live? How will she get money to live on? But Ed is not completely wrong either. It is unfair to expect him to shoulder all the burden just like that. None of this is his fault, really.

I ring Sadia while thinking all this. But she doesn't pick up. What happened? Did her family come again? Are her entire family a bunch of thugs? I should go home now. Nothing is going to happen here anyway…no class, no labs. There is no point lingering here.

But I am surprised as I enter into our apartment. Matt and Sadia are chatting and laughing heartily. Sadia is wearing a nice, new dress. She has freshened up and is looking great. She sees me staring at her dress and says, "How is it? Isn't it Nice? We went shopping. Matt bought it for me. I didn't have anything with me. So, he acted like a generous gentleman."

Sadia sounds happy and coy.

"You could have borrowed a few clothes from me. We're roughly the same size," I remind her.

"You can't borrow everything, can you? Underwear?" Matt winks.

"Sod off, Matt!" Sadia is bashful.

"Didn't you go to work, Matt?" I ask.

"Couldn't take the risk, Sri! What if they come again? To enquire about my 'girlfriend?'" Matt smiles again.

"Shut up Matt!" Sadia is laughing.

Suddenly I start feeling very dejected and exhausted. I have been worrying to death about Sadia, and here she is, all dolled up, chatting, and flirting with Matt. Why did I even bother to fight with Ed for her sake? If their relationship is so flimsy, why did she make such a big fuss about it?

"What happened, Sri? Are you alright?" Matt asks. He finally took the time to look at me.

"I'm fine. I called Sadia. She didn't pick up. So, I was getting worried. Didn't know that you were home, though."

"Did you call me? I didn't see. Maybe we were cooking in the kitchen then. Matt is such an amazing cook." Sadia seems to find everything about Matt amazing. She didn't even ask anything about Ed. Just then her phone rings again.

"Just a sec… It's Ed. I'll be back in a minute." She goes inside.

"OK, Sri, since you're back now, I can probably leave." Matt says.

"OK. Thanks for looking after Sadia."

"She is your friend, Sri. I have got to take care of her! Anyway, I didn't do much. Yesterday, that friend of yours, from MI6, he really helped. Seems, he takes great care of you. Did you speak to him after last night?"

"Yes. I met him at college."

"In your college?" Matt seems surprised.

"Yes. Another professor got killed this morning."

"Holy shit! Another one?"

"Yes, Matt. Our professors are dropping like autumn leaves." I reply coldly.

"Would you care to tell me in detail? What happened?"

"Well… what can I say! Thank God that Neil Basu is your close friend," says Matt, after listening to the details.

"He is just an acquaintance, Matt!" I protest.

"No, he isn't! You fancy him, don't you? Good choice."

Matt's words are exactly the same as Neil's yesterday.

Great! Matt thinks I fancy Neil and Neil thinks I fancy Matt. Wonderful.

None of them have said who they fancy, though!

Where does it leave me then? In no man's land of course!

Malabika Ray

# *The Poisoned Chalice*

A few days have passed since Helena's death. Classes have resumed. Labs have also been re-opened, except for the condensed matter and spectroscopy labs. There has not been any official confirmation on the cause of death either for Reza or for Helena. Everyone in the department is still sad and shocked. Prof. Yunis, our dean, is having a hard time finding replacement teachers to take the classes. A visiting professor, Professor Okuwele, is temporarily standing in for Helena. Prof. Kowalski will take charge of Reza's lab when it opens tomorrow.

Sadia and I have decided to go to Hounslow after the class today. Sadia wanted to meet her sister and check if there is any possibility for her getting a place there. When we went there in the evening, they gave the really good news that there will be a vacancy in a couple of weeks.

She is staying with me for now. She has also started working part time in a supermarket. It is not easy to do the evening shifts after college. I admire hire courage and resilience. Both she and her sister have also applied for state benefit. Neil is helping to speed up the vetting process there.

Farida looks happy to meet us. Poor thing, she is so young, must have been difficult for her to leave the house and family like this. But I am glad to see that she is coping well. She has even made friends with her roommate and a few more occupants. Her college is a bit far from Hounslow, but she is attending there regularly. Her teachers and friends are helping her a lot. That's good, because she now must do well in her studies to get a decent job after finishing her degree. That is the only way to get out of this mess. The same applies to Sadia as well, but then she already is a bright student, and it is only a matter of time before she bags a good job after finishing her Masters in the next nine months.

The three of us chat for a while and then we decide to visit the Primark nearby. Both Sadia and Farida are in dire need for some cheap clothes. I could do with some shopping, too. I live on scholarship, so I do not have much left in my pocket either after paying for rent, food, phone, and transport. Hence, Primark is also my go-to place for regular shopping.

But as soon as we step outside the charity building, we see Neil standing on the pavement, his car parked on the side.

"Hi! How are you? I came to check how you are doing. Is everything OK?" Neil asks the sisters. That's nice of him, though. He didn't have to check on them, yet he did. Maybe he is not a bad person after all.

"Yes, everything is fine, Mr. Basu. Thank you very much for finding this for us. They will have another vacancy soon and I can also move in here. I have spoken to them already," Sadia replies.

"That's really nice! You two will be able to stay together. But until then you are staying with Sri, I suppose?"

"Yes, I am. Sri has been a true friend. She has a big heart." Sadia smiles.

"I suppose so! Anyway, Ms. Marp…I mean Sri, do you have a moment now? I wanted to talk to you about something."

Seems I have to give up on my shopping plan today. I bid Sadia and Farida goodbye and go to a Starbucks with Neil.

"Before you ask me anything, I have a few questions for you," I say, as soon as we sit down with our coffees.

"Shoot!" Neil gives me permission.

"Number one. Did you check Reza's social media account? Did he get involved in any recent political movement or activism?"

"Spot on, Sri! You are on the right track. Reza was a big and vocal supporter of the activists who were protesting against the morality police in Iran after the death of Masha Amini in their custody. His Facebook and Twitter feed is full of posts supporting the protesters."

"Yes, I had the same impression when I talked to him," I agree.

## Alpha Beta Gamma

I was of course closely following the protest movements in Tehran and other parts of Iran last autumn, when their morality police brutally beat and killed Masha Amini, a twenty-two-year-old student, for not wearing the hijab in a proper way. A few strands of hair were apparently showing from under her headscarf, and she had to die because of that. She was the same age as me. There were waves of big protest at Tehran University where the protesters defied the authoritarian regime to voice their concerns. One day I spoke to Reza about it, too.

"You know Sri, it was not like this always. We used to have a much freer society. But in 1979, after the revolution, headscarves became mandatory for women. And since then, we are just going backwards, it seems." Reza lamented. I could see he was shaken by the whole event.

"And you know what, Masha is not the only victim. They have detained a lot and tortured many others who dared to protest. Some of them even died. I happen to know a few cases like this personally," he said in a sad tone.

It is always like this, I could not help thinking. Always others will decide what women should or should not wear, what they should or should not do, say, or think.

"Did you speak to Reza about his activism?" Neil's question brings me back to present.

"Not his activism, per se. But when these protests were going on full swing last year, and they detained a bunch of activists, then one day we got into the discussion. You see, I do have strong interests in feminist movements all over the world." I smile.

"I see. So, what did Reza say?"

"We discussed Masha's death, of course, in the custody of the morality police there. Reza was very worked up by the incident. You see, Neil, what struck me that day was that, even though he was forced to leave Iran thirty-two years ago, yet he still felt a strong connection with that country. He was still very much concerned about the people there and was on top of what is happening there. He was a very strong, opinionated person with an active moral compass."

"Yes, he was. Probably he had to pay a heavy price for that, with his life. Perhaps the government there was still thinking of him as a potential threat," Neil comments.

"But does any foreign government, however rogue or nasty, send spy-killers because of some social media posts?"

"No, they do not," Neil admits.

"So why is MI6 involved? Why are you checking for radiation? Why do you think it is not a 'simple' murder?"

I ask all these questions, which have been bothering me from day one, and for which I am yet to get any satisfactory answers.

Neil does not answer immediately, but sits quietly for a moment, sipping his latte. Then he speaks slowly, "Do you know anything about investigative journalism, Sri?"

"Investigative journalism? Y-yes… I mean I know the basics of course. Sometimes the journalists investigate a potential scandal or cover up. They act like sleuths, talk to their secret sources, and sometime uncover really big things."

"Any examples?" Neil asks smiling.

"Well, there is of course the Watergate, which finally brought President Nixon down."

"Any recent ones?" Neil is still smiling.

"Recent… I think Edward Snowden's revelations," I reply.

"Very good. Where were they published? The Snowden dossier?"

"In the New York Times and in the Guardian, perhaps? Right?"

"Right. The Guardian has a bit of a reputation for this. Recently, one of their journalists, Mary Mason, got an anonymous tip that the tipper has gotten hold of some documents from an ex-Iranian spy. These documents can potentially prove a lot of malpractice of their government. Even some conclusive proofs of Asad's alleged use of Sarin gas in Syria."

"Didn't the journalist, Mary Mason, ask why the ex-spy would give those bombshell documents to her?"

"Yes, she did and here it gets really interesting. The ex-spy, Nasser Ali, had a daughter, Sara, who was a bit of an activist. She was protesting against the atrocities of the morality police in Tehran last autumn, after Masha's death, when she was detained, brutally beaten and eventually she died in their custody, very much like Masha Amin."

"So now this ex-spy, Nasser Ali, turned into an aggrieved father after losing his beloved daughter Sara, and wants to take revenge on the government by exposing them, right?"

I finally understood the plot.

"Exactly." Neil nods.

"But how did Nasser Ali contact Guardian's Mary Mason? Did he contact her from Iran?" I ask this because I thought it would be too risky to contact a European Newspaper from Iran to share anti-government information. Even though all these newspapers use secret servers to get anonymous tips, it would still be a huge risk to take within an authoritarian regime like Iran.

"No, he did not contact the Guardian directly, that would be suicidal. This ex-spy, Nasser Ali, contacted someone in London, who was also of Iranian origin and was very critical of the government there. Nasser Ali sent his evidence and documents to this London based person, who finally tipped off The Guardian anonymously," Neil explains.

"I see. And you think this person who tipped off Guardian was Reza? And that information somehow got leaked and he was killed as a result?"

"Well, at least that's a theory, Ms. Marple, a plausible one," Neil smiles.

"Why do you always call me Ms. Marple?" I finally ask.

"That's a compliment! Aren't you happy?"

"What compliment? Am I that old? Do I knit like her? Gossip like her?" I ask angrily.

"Age is just a number and knitting and gossiping are not her main traits, Sri! Her main characteristic is that she can solve mysteries just by analytical deduction. Without chasing the criminals or getting into fist fights with them directly. Not physical, but purely cerebral detection. This suits a sloppy sleuth like you perfectly!"

Neil smiles. But I replied with a stern face, "I am neither sloppy nor a sleuth."

"You are sloppy, Ms. Marple, obviously! Look, you just dropped one of your gloves on the floor." Neil points his finger at the floor, under my chair where one of my brown gloves is lying. Just as I bend down to pick it up, my phone rolls out of my pocket and falls on the floor. Neil picks it up, gives it back to me and says, "So, you have already demonstrated your sloppiness quite successfully. Now let's test your sleuthing skill. Come with me." Neil gets up from his chair.

"Where to?"

"To the morgue."

"M-Morgue? W-why?" I was not quite expecting this.

"How can you be a sleuth if you get so squeamish at the mere mentioning of the word morgue! You can't really do much sleuthing from the armchair in your garden these days, Ms. Marple. The world has changed."

"B-But, whose body? Reza's or…?" I am still trying to process this information.

"Helena's. Reza's body is also kept in the morgue, but you won't be able to see it."

"W-what do you mean?"

"Do you have any idea how a dead body kept in the morgue for weeks looks like? Smells like? The older they are, more difficult they become to handle, even for the seasoned professionals. For a newbie like you, let's start with a fresher body."

"You sound morbid. And gross."

"Welcome to the real-world investigation, Sri! As a senior in this line of work, let me give you a piece of advice. Things are about to get nasty, a hell of a lot more nasty. So, brace yourself for it."

# Alpha Beta Gamma

Neil and I enter the morgue at the University College hospital at around eight in the evening. A security guard at the morgue and Mr. Duncan Smith from the Met police are also there with us. The heavy metal door is closed behind us as we enter the cold room. The room has barren white walls, grey parquet floors and is lit by bright white light. The wall at the far end is stacked with metal lockers, just as I have seen in so many Hollywood movies. Now this is real. Very, very real.

The security guard went ahead and pulled a locker out. Helena's body is lying on the cold slab. The autopsy has already been done. The skin of the body is white, very white, like paper. The lips are dark blue, almost black. Her palms are kept across her chest, her fingers…

…My stomach is churning… I am feeling sick. I put my hand over my mouth, my body gives an involuntary jerk. Duncan is saying something… but I can't hear him… there is a ringing noise in my ears. Neil is coming towards me—

I don't remember anything else.

\*\*\*

I wake up in a semi dark, unfamiliar room. Waking up is like emerging from a thick fog. As my eyes flutter open to the dimly lit room, the details slowly come into focus. The ceiling is higher than I am used to, adorned with unfamiliar patterns. The air feels cooler, carrying a faint scent of something I can't quite place.

I blink, trying to piece together how I have ended up here. The last thing I remember is a rush of dizziness, the world spinning before everything went black in that morgue. Now, I find myself lying in this unfamiliar but comfortable bed, draped in white sheets.

As I sit up, my head pounds with a dull ache. I notice the room's decor is minimalistic but elegant, with sleek furniture and neutral colours. A single window allows a sliver of sunlight to peek through, casting a gentle glow on the polished wooden floor. I glance around, searching for any clues to my whereabouts. A nightstand beside the bed holds a glass of water. I still feel a little dizzy, but otherwise fine. I sit up on the bed and switch the lights on. Neil enters the room.

"So, Ms. Marple, feeling better?" he asks.
"Where am I?" I want to ask the cliché question but did not. Neil is wearing different clothes now. Could this be his apartment then?
"This must be your home. I can see that you have changed." I comment.
"Good. You can speak and can also do deductions again. That's nice. I must say, you are the undisputed champion in sleuthing from bed."
"Stop talking nonsense. How did I end up in your bed?" I demand to know.

"Look, how a beautiful girl like you ended up in the bed of a handsome guy like me, can have many interesting answers…"

"Is it your hobby to embarrass people? Do you get some sort of sadistic pleasure out of it?"

"Blimey! I am saying all this because I did not want to embarrass you. Wouldn't you be more embarrassed if I told you the truth? That you threw up on me and passed out in the morgue twenty seconds after staring at Helena's dead body?"

Shit! I am so very embarrassed, indeed! Throwing up and passing out, any one of them would have been embarrassing enough. But I somehow managed to do both. What a shame. And I call myself a sleuth? Can anyone imagine Sherlock Holmes passing out looking at a dead body? Or Poirot throwing up in the morgue? I am not a sloppy sleuth, I am just plain, old sloppy.

"Don't be so harsh on yourself, Sri! It is normal," says Neil in a soft voice.

"It's fine. You don't have to console me. Did it happen to you when you went to the morgue for the first time?" I ask grumpily.

"No, but afterwards, I could not eat anything for three days. Thanks to that lingering, combined smell of formaldehyde, sanitizers, and dead flesh," says Neil with a wry smile. "When I saw my first dead body… it was a week old, maggot ridden, rotten body in the attic of an abandoned flat… I threw up on my supervisor. So, see, I am not that far behind!" Neil continues. "This is a real world crime scene, Sri, not a suspense thriller on Netflix. No matter how gory a scene they show, they can never carry the smell to the viewers, and the smell IS the biggest assault on your senses."

He pauses for a while and then speaks again.

"Sleuths or spies are also human beings, Sri. They make mistakes and at times they also get mighty scared. They get tired, they get stressed and they do feel like throwing up at the stench of rotting flesh." Neil finally stops

"Still, you never passed out. Did you?" I ask.

"No, I didn't. But my sister had that experience when she saw her first dead body." Neil smiles.

"Do you have a sister? Is she in the police, too?"

"Half-sister, actually, my mum and Kevin's child. No, she is not in the police. She just started studying medicine, in Glasgow. Just like you, she also passed out after looking at a dead body on the dissection table. Perhaps it is a woman thing!"

"What did you say?" I ask angrily.

"There you are, back in your feminist form! Good. Now please come and eat something."

"No, thanks, but I will go home now," I protest.

"Do you know what time it is?" asked Neil.

"No, what time is it?"

"11:37 PM. Stay here. You can go home tomorrow morning. It will not be the end of the world if you can't check your handsome flatmate out for a day. You can compensate for it tomorrow by ogling at him twice as much!"

Neil is trying to be obnoxious again, but I can see that he is making sense. It would be a lot of hassle to go back to my apartment at this hour now. Moreover, I am not feeling one hundred percent fit either. Hence, I agree.

"Ok! But I need to call Matt then…"

"Already taken care of. I called him and explained the situation in brief."

"Thanks! Is this your guest room?"

"A junior detective like me doesn't get paid very much, Sri. There is only one bedroom in this apartment." Neil smiles.

"Then… how?"

"If you think that I will spend the night in this room taking care of you, then you are grossly mistaken. There is a futon in the living room, I will sleep there. If you go to the bathroom in the night, then please try not to confuse my sleeping body with another dead body and pass out again!"

Next morning, I leave Neil's apartment after breakfast. I'm feeling a lot better now. So, I thank him and leave for my apartment to change my clothes and freshen up before heading for Uni. When I reach home, I find both Matt and Sadia there.

"Good morning, Sri! How are you?" Matt greets me.

"Morning! I am fine. What about you? Any more visits from Sadia's family?" I enquire.

"No, thankfully not. I think Neil's scared them off, at least for now." Matt smiles and then says, "Oh, by the way, Sri, some aunt of yours called on the landline yesterday…"

"Who? Aunt Shukla?" I ask.

"Yep, that's the one. She apparently couldn't reach you on your mobile so called here to check if everything was fine."

Perhaps she called when I was senseless.

"Did she leave any message?"

"Nothing in particular. Asked me where you were. Don't worry, I told her that you were with you date and would be back in morning, so nothing to worry—"

"What? What did you say? That I was with my date last night?"

"Were you not? But Neil called and told me that you are with him." Matt seems confused.

"Since when is Neil my date?"

"Blimey! That's what I thought, actually, from your body language… isn't it, Sadia?"

Matt looks at Sadia for confirmation. Sadia has been smiling all along. Now she nods and says, "One hundred percent!"

"Jesus! You know what, you two also look like a couple, from your body language. You two were also alone here, in this apartment, last night. Are you two dating?" I snap.

"What are you talking about, Sri? Have you lost your mind?" Sadia sounds a little annoyed.

"Yes, I have lost my mind, OK? Neil says that I should date Matt and Matt dictates that I should go out with Neil. It is my life, for God's sake. So, let me decide! Did I ask any one of you to go out with me? Why are you then passing me around like a hot potato?"

I storm to my room and bang the door closed, leaving an utterly perplexed Matt and Sadia behind.

This is so annoying. Matt has no idea, but I know what's going to happen now. Aunt Shukla, the gossip Reuters will spread the news faster than the speed of light. First, my mum, then all other relatives, friends… everyone will know that Sri is dating some random guy and all hell will break lose. I already have a thousand things to worry about; the exam is round the corner, I have pending assignments, experiments… and now this: completely uncalled for, really.

My phone starts ringing within five minutes.

"Yes, mum…"

"Sri, pack your things now. You will go to Shukla's in the evening. For good. I already told her." Mum's voice is sombre.

"What! Why?"

"You know why, Sri. Shukla offered to let you stay in her spare room, free of cost. So generous, God bless her. It's good for you, too. Give this flat up, you will save a lot of money."

"Are you completely out of your mind, mum? Will I commute to Queen Mary from Wimbledon every day? Do you have any idea how long that will take?"

"You can find something nearby later—like a girls' hostel or that sort of thing. Now listen to me and do as I say—"

"No mum! You listen to me. This is not Kolkata, you don't get chaperoned girls' hostels. Girls here live where they want to, with whomever they want."

"There are many such girls in Kolkata, too. Who live how they want to, without heeding to any social norms. But you better listen to our advice—"

"No mum! You listen to me. I am not a child, I am twenty-three. I live here on my own scholarship money. It's my life and I should decide what's best for me—"

"I wish you knew what is best for you, Sri! We also dated—your baba and me. But we always knew we were going to be married. We never dreamt of going out with multiple random guys like this—"

"So? You just got lucky. Or perhaps unlucky, I don't know—depends on your point of view, I suppose. That the first ever relationship worked for you. It does not have to be like that for everyone, does it? Some people may have to weigh their options before settling down."

"What is that supposed to mean? Will you now explore the field?"

"Why not? You explore hundred shops before buying a sari worth five thousand rupees. This is a much bigger decision, why should I not weigh my options?"

"What? Will you now go out with a hundred—" mum sounded alarmed.

"It's a figure of speech, Ma, metaphorical. You know what I mean!"

"—I can't deal with this girl anymore. You better talk to her. You're the one who pampered and spoiled her like this—" mum handed the phone over to baba.

"Sri, my child! How are you, darling? Were you not home last night?" Baba asks in a cheerful voice.

"I am fine, Baba. Actually, something urgent came up last night, so I had to—"

"—She is lying, you see! Her flatmate told Shukla that she was with her date last night. What a shame! Shukla told me that her children, who were born and brought up in London, never would do such things. And here is my daughter, after spending barely a year there, has started living such a reckless life. I had to listen to all of Shukla's insinuations—" mum sounds properly indignant.

"Baba, tell mum that I have no intention of following the footsteps of Aunt Shukla's children. The daughter, Rikta, wears tons of makeup and snaps pouty selfies the whole day. And the boy, Riju, can't keep a job for more than two months. Between them they have never read a single book outside their school curriculum. And most importantly, no one has a say on what I shall eat, what I shall wear or who I shall sleep with—"

"—Listen! Just listen to her! Such an insolent girl." I can hear mum's angry voice.

"—Leave it to me, please. I am speaking to her, am I not? Sri, mind your language, sweetheart—" Baba's voice again.

"Sorry Baba."

"Look, I have complete faith in your judgement. I know you will not take a rash decision."

"Thank you, Baba. Just tell mum that if I want to sleep around then—"

## Alpha Beta Gamma

"Spare me the details, Sri! I don't want to know. Take your time, do your experimentation or exploration all you want. Just let me know when you finally converge, if you do it at all, that is. I'll then talk to the priest. Before that, just keep me out of it."

"He-he. You and priest, Baba? Did you ever set foot in a temple? Or talk to the priest? Granny always scolds you, doesn't she?"

"So what? I can talk to a priest if I want to! There is a first time for everything, you see! Just let me know when you are ready. In about five years? What do you say?"

"Make it seven, Baba!"

"Done."

A chat with Baba always lifts my spirit up. No one understand me like him. I miss him so much! Anyway, I don't have to move to Aunt Shukla's just yet. What a great relief. Now I have to get ready and go to college.

When I reach college, all of these thoughts obviously went out of my head; there are back-to-back classes—mathematical physics, optics, and the fluid dynamics. For the next four hours, my brain is fully engaged in tensors, Fermat's principle, and Euler's equation.

When the classes finally end, I am feeling ravenous and head straight to the canteen. Holding my tray, as I am trying to find a free table, I see Roberto and Vignesh sitting at a table in the corner. Roberto is Reza's PhD student and Vignesh was doing his post-doc with Reza. I go to their table, smile, and asked if I can join them.

"Yes, of course. Please sit." Roberto smiles back.

"Thanks! How is your research going, Roberto?" I ask.

"It was going great, Sri. But now it seems I need to find a new advisor," says Roberto in a grim voice.

"Yeah, of course. Will you work with prof. Kowalski now?" I ask because Kowalski is the other condensed matter professor in our department.

"Hell, no! My work is highly computational. And professor Kowalski cannot write a computer program to save his life." Roberto smiles. Both Vignesh and I join him. Professor Kowalski's computer knowledge, or the lack of it, is a steady source of jokes among the students.

"I think I will work with Professor Yunis," Roberto says.

"Professor Yunis? Does he have time? He seems to be always busy with administrative work." I comment.

"That's true. He is the dean, after all. It will be a challenge for both me and Roberto," Vignesh agrees with me.

"By the way, were any of you working late that day? That day… when, you know, Reza was killed?" I ask innocently.

"No, not me. I left at five o'clock sharp," Roberto replies.

"Well. I stayed up until eight thirty, but I was not in his lab. I was working at our postdocs' office. But why do you ask, Sri? Do you suspect us to be the murderers?" Vignesh asks with a smile.

"Oh, no, no. Not at all. I was thinking maybe you were working on some paper together, that's why he had to stay in the lab at night," I clarify hastily.

"No, Sri, Reza was not working on any paper right now. Roberto has just joined, he is not in a position to write any paper yet. And Reza and I already submitted our last paper a few weeks back. Nothing was in the queue when… I mean… that incident happened." Vignesh clarifies.

That's weird, I think. Because Irene, Reza's wife clearly said he was very busy working and also talked about some 'deadline' and 'submission'. But neither Roberto nor Vignesh knew of any such impending deadline. Why did he have to work so late in the lab that day then? What kept him occupied in his last days?"

My train of thoughts are stopped by Sadia when she comes to join me at the table. It's almost two o'clock and the canteen is already looking a bit deserted. Roberto and Vignesh had left a few minutes back.

"What's the matter with you, Sri? Are you jealous about Matt? Are you two into each other?" Sadia asks me point blank.

"No. I have nothing with Matt. Or anyone else, for that matter."

"So, what was that this morning? That outburst? It seems you are hiding something from me."

"I have the same feeling, Sadia, feels like you are hiding something from me. What's with you and Ed?"

"Nothing. Ed got a little scared. Can't blame him, really."

"Do you guys want to marry?"

"Are you mad? We are just twenty-three, still students, without a stable job."

"What are your plans, then? Will you go back home?"

"What for? To get butchered?"

"Then how long will you continue like this?"

"I know I am imposing on you. But please bear with me for a few more days. If you ask, Matt will definitely agree to let me stay."

"He will let you stay even if I don't ask."

"What is that supposed to mean?"

"Nothing."

The golden locks on the buttery-smooth skin of the bare back, over the snake tattoo, flash through my mind.

"Did you stay at Neil's yesterday?" Sadia asks.
"Yes."
"Why? You are getting jealous if someone comes close to Matt and at the same time spending the night at Neil's—"
"So what? Do I have to explain it to you? Should I seek your permission?" I sound angry and bitter.
"No, you don't have to, sorry. I am grateful that you let me stay at your place. Anyway, let's go. We have to be in the condensed matter lab soon."

I feel bad. She is my closest friend here and she needs me. Why am I being so snappy? Before I can say anything, Sadia starts walking without me.

The next three hours pass quickly as I am engrossed in the work in the condensed matter lab. It is good though, all those silly thoughts go out of my head. Work helps best to bring a disturbed mind back on track. Finally, after finishing the work, I feel like having a cup of coffee.

There is a small pantry inside, right at the entrance of this lab. Nothing fancy, just a kettle, a coffee machine, a few teabags on the counter and a few cups and mugs in the overhead cupboards. As I stand in front of the counter, I can't help thinking of Reza. He was lying right here, at the door between this pantry and the main lab. Then Helena's dead body at the morgue came to my head again. I smell the strong coffee beans to push back those feelings of being sick again.

This is good coffee. Lavazza. Reza didn't drink much coffee though; he was a tea person. He used to keep his own little teapot of Moroccan design, right beside the electric kettle. He used to make his own tea in that and kept drinking it the whole time. He used to top it up as needed. It was his very own teapot, no one else used it. Now it's there, on the counter. Empty. Who would fill it up now?

As I am pouring coffee in my mug, a thought strikes me like a lightning bolt. Reza was poisoned, right? What if…?

I leave my mug and run towards the Nuclear Physics lab. Ed is working there. He is surprised to see me and asks, "What's the matter Sri? Why are you panting?"

"Nothing… give me a Geiger from that shelf. Now!" I point to the rack behind Ed.

"Why?" Ed is still very surprised.

"I need it. Give it to me, quick!"

I snatch the Geiger counter from a stunned Ed's hand and come back running to the condensed matter lab again. Now Sadia and Luiza are there in the pantry. They are making tea together. I push them aside.

"Move! Move! Give me some space." I say hastily.

"What's this, Sri? Wait a little, please." Sadia sounds vexed.

"No time to wait. Move."

I shove them aside and started measuring the radiation in that teapot with the Geiger. Then I measure it elsewhere in the room.

It is exactly as I thought. The radiation level is higher inside the teapot compared to nearby areas. Not dangerously higher, but still distinctly higher.

Sadia and Luiza are also watching me keenly now. They have given up on making their tea.

"D-Does that mean… In that teapot…?" Luiza starts stammering.

"Yes, you saw it yourself, didn't you? Higher level of radiation inside."

"Did they use it to… to kill Reza?" Sadia swallows hard.

"That I am not so sure of. Still, we should inform the police, I think."

"But… The radiation level is not fatally high." Luiza sounds doubtful.

"No. But remember, we are seeing this after two weeks. So—"

"—So, depending on the half-life of the radioactive substance used, it could be much lower now than that day." Luiza understands it right.

The half-life of a radioactive substance determines how quickly it will lose its potency. If a substance has a half-life of two days, say, then after two days it will lose half its strength, after four days one fourth of its strength and so on and so forth. So essentially, after two weeks, its strength will be reduced substantially.

"What should we do now?" asks Sadia.
"We have to inform the police. Let me go outside and call Neil. But don't touch the teapot. I'll be back in a sec—"
"Hello girls! Could you please stop gossiping and start concentrating on your work instead?"
Prof. Kowalski is standing right behind us. He is known to be somewhat dismissive towards women.
"We were not gossiping, professor. Actually, Sri found a—ouch!" Luiza lets out a muffled cry as I pinch her hard on her elbow.
"Yes? What about Sri?" Prof. Kowalski squints his eyes.
"N-nothing professor. Actually, my date, Neil, was supposed to take me out to the dinner tonight. That's why… can I go outside for a sec, professor? Please?"
"Why?" The professor still sounds suspicious.

"We originally planned to meet here, at the campus, after the lab. But Sadia and Luiza just reminded me that I won't have the opportunity to change into something nice then. So, I will just call him to pick me up from my apartment instead. I will be back in a jiffy, professor, I promise."

I play the part of lovelorn young girl quite convincingly, I suppose.

"Do whatever you want to do." Prof. Kowalski sounds rather vexed. "But I must warn you that you can't do physics like this. It requires dedication—what is this Geiger doing here?" asks the professor, pointing at the instrument lying on the counter, beside the coffee machine. Well, this will be hard to explain. People usually don't need a Geiger in the condensed matter lab. But before I could come up with something, Sadia leaped to my defence.

"This… I think Ed has left it here. He is working in the nuclear lab today. Just came here to meet me a while ago. He must have left it here."

Now it's Sadia's turn to play the lovestruck, vain girl.

"See, what I mean? This is all you girls do all the time; boyfriends and dates and makeup and whatnot. Hopeless. Can't do physics like this, I am telling you."

Sexist professor Kowalski shakes his head and goes inside. Hopefully he did not suspect anything. I mutter a thanks to Sadia and go outside. Standing at the department's entrance, I call Neil, but he doesn't pick up. I give up after three tries, leaving a voice message for him.

But what kind of radioactive substance could it be? I keep thinking. Something that can decay to a much lower strength within two weeks. That means it must have a half-life of just a few days. Should I Google it, or should I go to the library? But half-life may not be the only criteria, there could be other physical and chemical properties. It would be nice to consult a Chemist.

Matt! Yes, Matt. He has a background in Chemistry. Perhaps he can help me. Let me call him.

Thankfully Matt picks up the phone just after two rings.
"What's up Sri? Is everything alright? Sadia?"
Wow! Matt seems to be mighty concerned about Sadia. But I force those silly thoughts away. I have a lot more important thing to discuss with him.

"Yes, everything is alright. Actually, I wanted to check something with you."
"Regarding what?"

"About the radioactive substances and their properties. Half-life, say, a few days. But potential poison, deadly poison. Any idea what it could be?"

"Is this related to the murder of your professor that day?"

"Maybe, but I am not very sure at the moment."

"Wait, Sri. Where are you calling from? Public place?"

"Yes, I am standing in our campus, in front of our main building."

"Then stop. Don't talk about it now." Matt is firm.

"Why?"

"Two people have already been murdered, Sri. Don't take risks."

"OK. So, let us talk in the evening when we are both back home."

"I won't be back tonight, I am afraid. I will stay with Simran."

"Oh! Then?"

I did not want to wait too long to find the answers.

"Are you free now? Can you come over to Mayfair?" Matt asks.

"Mayfair? Why?"

"I will be there at a restaurant in about an hour. You can join me there. I am sending you the location."

"But a restaurant in Mayfair, must be very expensive!"

I obviously have to think what I can afford and what I cannot.

"The dinner is on me." Matt offers generously.

"No Matt. Let's talk tomorrow."

I do not like taking favours from others.

"You can pay me back after getting a job. Or from the prize money that you will receive after solving this case!" says Matt in a lighter tone.

"There is no prize money for solving this case, Matt. Will you have a date with you at the restaurant?"

"No. The only girl with me there will be you." Matt laughs.

"But I am not wearing anything fancy. They will throw me out of a posh restaurant if I turn up there in my worn-out jeans and crumpled T."

"Your denim jeans and the purple top, right? The ones that you were wearing in the morning? You look gorgeous in them. Don't hesitate, just come over."

Wow, I myself forgot which colour top I am wearing. I am a sloppy sleuth indeed. But am I a sleuth? For real? Whatever! Enough of these self-doubts, I have to drop by the library at once and then will head for Mayfair straight away.

As soon as I enter into the Mayfair restaurant, I know that I have never been to a place this fancy. The place is full of well-dressed people. Not everyone is wearing formalwear, though, some are even wearing jeans. But those are expensive jeans, not the cheap, Primark ones, like me. The waiter shows me a to corner table at the far end of the restaurant. Matt is already sitting there, dressed impeccably in Levi jeans and a Lacoste T. He smiles and waves at me.

"So, what do you prefer, Sri," Matt asks as he passes the drinks menu to me.
"Prosecco."
Matt calls the waiter, orders the drink, and then asks, "Now tell me, what's the matter."

"You should have talked to the Police Sri. They need to examine the teapot," Matt says after listening to the whole teapot story from me.
"I called Neil. But he is not picking up." I confess.
"Maybe he is on holiday. Or in a secret meeting. You could have called the local police station."
"Was thinking about it, but then I thought, these radiation poisoning theories… not sure if the local police would take me seriously or just laugh at me."
"Hmm, you may have a point there. What do you want from me?" Matt asks.

"Do you have any idea what this poison could be? I mean you studied Chemistry, so I thought perhaps you could help."

"You said the radiation level inside the teapot was high, but not fatally high, right?"

"Yes, Matt. Slightly higher than the surrounding, but not alarming," I explain.

"Well, basically, then you need something with a half-life of a few days. Because only that would explain the reduced level of radiation within a couple of weeks." Matt understands it correctly.

"Yes, Matt. I Googled it. But that is a very long list, of all these elements and their hundreds of isotopes that could fall in this range. It is way more difficult than finding a needle in a haystack; like finding a spaceship in andromeda galaxy."

"True, but Sri, I am not so sure that half-life is the only thing to be considered here."

"What do you mean, Matt?"

"I mean if there was indeed radioactive substance in the teapot, how come the police and MI6 missed it? They checked everything thoroughly with Geiger, didn't they?"

"Yes, they did," I have to admit. "But, perhaps, they somehow missed it," I say in an unsure way.

But Matt shakes his head and says, "As far as I can remember, an isotope of radium or uranium will be in that half-life range. But if that were the case, it should have been detected by the police Geiger Counters. If the teapot really contained even a tiny amount of radium or uranium, then the Geiger readings should have gone through the roof. Why just the teapot, I mean, there would have been crazy reading from the whole room and the corridor outside. There is no chance in hell that the police could have missed it."

Matt's arguments are strong, very strong.

"Hmm, you are right Matt. Here it seems very concentrated, within the teapot. But a higher reading, nevertheless, compared to the surrounding. How would you explain that?"

"Look Sri, you are only thinking of radiation. Why is that? What about other poisons and toxins? Radium or uranium are very bad murder weapons. They do not cause immediate death. It takes months, years even. Just think about Madame Curie, she was so badly exposed to radium; she used to touch pitch-blend with bare hands, for Christ's sake! Obviously, because no one knew about its harmful effects back then. But just think how many years it took for her to finally die of cancer, whereas Reza died within hours."

"What about thallium?" I ask, thinking of the postmortem report that Neil talked about. His boss Daniel seemed to be gravitating towards thallium.

"Thallium could be a possibility because its half-life will fall within that range—of a few days. But that is very old school. These days not much thallium is even synthesized." Matt explains.

"And thallium doesn't cause such instant death either, right?"

"No, it doesn't. It should take at least a few weeks or months to die from thallium poisoning."

"Yes. That's the part that is not matching with other evidence." I frown.

"Yes, Sri. There are many missing pieces in this puzzle. By the way, why did you ask about thallium?"

"Neil's boss, Daniel, suspects it," I say.

"Neil's boss? Senior detective in MI6? That's really weird! He should know better." Matt seems surprised.

"Well, Neil said he is very old school."

"Could be. There is bureaucracy everywhere, I suppose. Anyway, my suggestion would be, Sri, you better contact Neil. If you can't get hold of him in the work phone, then try his private phone." Matt suggests.

"I don't have his private number, Matt."

"Strange!"

"Why strange?"

"You just spent last night together!"

"Rich coming from you, Matt. Don't you bring a new girl home every other week?"

"I do. But I normally do have their numbers with me," Matt smiles.

"Jesus! Doesn't you phone memory get full?"

"Don't know about my phone's memory, but my memory definitely gets full. You know what I did the other day? I called Casey Gina… in bed! Just think about it. Such a mess." Matt starts laughing heartily and I can't help joining him.

But suddenly the smile gets wiped away from his face. He is looking at the door. I follow his gaze and see a well-dressed Neil entering into the restaurant. He is not alone. His right hand is wrapped around the waist of a gorgeous girl in a black cocktail dress. A tall girl, slim, with long, dark brown hair, very long nails painted nicely on her manicured hands.

"Oh, that explains it! He is on a date and that is why not picking up the work phone." I say in a normal voice as I empty the prosecco glass.

Malabika Ray

# *Scavenging the Truth*

Today I came early to the department. Last night Neil introduced us to his date in the restaurant. Her name was Anthea. I finished half a bottle of red after they had gone to their reserved table. I might have finished the full bottle if Matt had not intervened. He offered to come back home with me, cancelling his plan for the evening. I protested strongly. I am not a delicate lily and I do not need a bodyguard to accompany me all the time. Enough of these two hunks' mixed signals. But Matt insisted on getting a taxi for me. A ride from Mayfair to Canning Town in a black cab would normally be unaffordable for a poor student like me, but Matt paid for it. Apparently, he would bill it as expenses to his agency.

I get up a little late this morning, but then get ready quickly. Sadia will come later. After arriving at college, I go straight to the condensed matter lab. The pantry is right by the entrance. There are coffee machines and tea bags on the counter as usual, but no sign of the teapot. Where is it?

Normally it is just standing there. Where did it vanish to? How strange! Right after that incident yesterday… very fishy. I start looking for it everywhere, in the cupboard, in the sink, on the tables nearby, even in the microwave. But no, it just vanished.

"Are you looking for something?"
Our Polish cleaner Natalia asks. She has just entered the room with her broom and mops.
"Yes, there used to be a teapot here, on the counter. A very colourful, nice one. Have you seen it?" I ask her.
"Professor Tavacol's teapot?" Natalia asks back.
"Yes, yes. Have you seen it?"
"It is broken, unfortunately." Natalia says.
"How? Did you break it?" I ask her.
"No! Why should I break it? I came in the morning to vacuum here and saw a small piece under the counter. Someone must have broken it yesterday and thrown it out. That was the only piece lying there on the floor."
Natalia seems a little offended at my suggestion that she broke the teapot.
"Who broke it?" I ask again.
"How should I know?" Natalia sounds vexed.
"What happened to that broken piece?" I keep asking.

"I emptied the trash in the morning. Everything went into the big wheelie bin outside." Natalia replies. She looks a bit surprised at my interrogation about a broken teapot.

But this is so strange! The teapot was lying there in the corner for all these years and just when I need it, it gets broken. Bad luck, indeed. But is it just bad luck or did someone break it on purpose? The whole thing looks so damn suspicious. I go outside for some fresh air.

"Sri!"
I turn around and see Neil. He is in regular jeans and shirt, not in last night's glam suit. This Neil looks more familiar, but I feel a strange sense of sadness and annoyance looking at him. Don't know why though. He is a single man and can go for a date if he wishes so. Anyway, no time to think about this stuff, I have a bigger problem at hand for which I need his help.

"Hi, Neil," I greet him.
"Have you lost your phone again?" he asks.
"My phone? No. It's right here, in my pocket." I take it out.
"So why don't you pick it up?" Neil asks sharply.
"Oh, it was on silent. I missed it. Did you try to call me?"
"Yes! At least a hundred times. After I got your voicemail," Neil says.
"Is that so? When did you get my message?"

"At about two in the morning. Didn't want to bother you then. I have been trying to get hold of you all morning, but you are not picking up," Neil complains.

His complaints suddenly made me angry. Why does he expect that I should take his call anytime of the day? Am I his subordinate? Do I work under him?

"I am a private citizen. I think it is no big deal if I do not pick up my phone every time minute of the day. Especially when you, an MI6 investigator—"

"—I was on leave yesterday, Sri. Even investigators occasionally need time off."

"I see! Was your holiday only until two in the morning? Why did you check your voice message then?"

"I… I was up then, actually…" Neil takes his eyes off me and starts stammering.

I understand very well what 'actually' has happened. That long, raw, reddish scratch mark on his neck, right above his shirt collar, was not caused by any enemy weapon. It was caused by nails, long nails, like those of Anthea. Neil's sharp eyes are following my gaze. I look away.

"What are you doing here?" I ask.

"What is the meaning of your voice message? Which teapot? What was the reading on the Geiger Counter?"

Neil is totally professional now. I describe everything in detail.

"Come, show me the teapot," he says, after listening to the whole story.
"Not possible. It is broken." I reply.
"What? How?"
I tell him what I heard from Natalia.

"Show me where your big wheelie bin is." Neil sounds determined.
"It's near the car park. There are five or six big bins out there, for general trash and recycling."
Neil has already started walking towards the car park. I stand there for a little while, then start following him.

"Are you planning on scavenging through the rubbish?"
I am astonished to see him taking out a pair of surgical gloves from his pocket, as we reached the wheelie bin containing the general rubbish.
"Yep."
"Are you serious? It's so dirty!" My nose twitches as he opens the lid of the bin. It is full of plastic bags containing waste from the entire college, from all departments and labs. The stench has already started to fill the air.
"If you wish to help, then this is the time, Ms. Marple."
Neil offers me another pair of gloves.

"Either put them on and help me, or stand aside. No point standing so close just to have a closer look, it is not a pretty sight, and the stench is strong. I don't want you to throw up on me again," says Neil in a matter-of-fact way.

Without saying another word, I take the gloves from Neil, put them on and start rummaging through the trash. After half an hour of digging through the garbage of the entire college, we find the sought-after treasure: the broken piece of the teapot. In the meantime, the security guards have come over and asked what we were doing scavenging the wheelie bin like this. But Neil brought the situation under control by showing his badge. They left us doing the 'police work'.

"Thank you, Sri, well done. I hope you had a great date last night," Neil comments as he puts the broken piece of ceramic in a plastic zip locked bag.
"My date?"
"Yes, with Matt, I mean."
"Stop, stop, stop! You have got to stop doing that. Both of you," I shout.
A couple of students are standing near a red Nissan. They turn their heads towards us.
"What? What should I stop. Sri? And what do you mean by 'both'?" Neil seemed genuinely surprised.

"I mean you and Matt. Both of you have to stop passing me like a hot potato. Listen very carefully. I am not dating either of you and I am not sleeping with either one of you. Clear?" I take a deep breath.

Neil is silent for a moment and then he speaks, "Well, at least I know one of those things already," he says in a low voice after a pause.

"Excuse me?"

"I mean I know that you are not sleeping with me!"

We look at each other for a while and then burst into loud laughter.

\*\*\*

"So, Ms. Marple, where does this leave us now?" asks Neil through a mouthful of pizza. After finishing the scavenging, he asked me if I would like to join him for an early lunch. Since I hadn't had any breakfast, I said yes. We are sitting at the same pizza place outside our college.

"Well, something must have been there in that teapot," I comment after swallowing the bite.

"What could it be? Such a deadly poison? Remember, the Geiger reading is high, but not fatal."

"True. Still, the reading is higher than the surroundings."

"Perhaps it is a red herring Sri, I don't know." Neil sounds unsure.

"The symptoms somewhat match with that of thallium poisoning. But do people die instantly from thallium?" I ask again.

"No, they don't. And it is not used very much these days." says Neil, just like Matt told me yesterday.

"But, if there was something in that teapot, how did Helena die? She didn't drink from that pot, did she?" I asked.

"Good that you mentioned it, Sri. About Helena… do you know why I took you to the morgue?" Neil asks me.

"No. You never told me. Except that I need to gain experience." I give a smile.

"Well that too; you can't be a real sleuth unless you visit a morgue. But that was not the only reason."

"What else then?"

"I wanted to show you her hair."

"Hair?" I did not see this coming, honestly.

"Yes. She had a bald patch on the top of her head. The doctor who did the autopsy did not suspect anything funny; could have been a normal bald patch, she was old after all—"

"Old or not, Helena was not bald. She had a headful of dense, salt and pepper hair," I say firmly.

"Are you sure? Could this then be an effect of some toxin?" Neil frowns.

"Could be. But how? How was Helena poisoned? She did not drink that poisoned tea, did she?"

"No. She must have been poisoned in some other way. But the same poison, but in some other way." The furrows on Neil's forehead deepen.

Suddenly a scene from the morgue flashed through my mind.

"Finger. Helena's forefinger!" I shout. Neil looks utterly confused. "That day, in the morgue, I saw a small cut on Helena's finger. Small, but deep cut." I explain excitedly.'

"Wow! I am impressed. So, you did observe something important in those twenty seconds prior to throwing up and passing out? Amazing!" says Neil, mockingly, but he soon comes back to his serious self as I give him a dirty look. "Brilliant, Ms. Marple. A cut means direct connection with the bloodstream. Helena somehow must have touched that poison, which came in direct contact with her blood and had an immediate, catastrophic effect." Neil summarises it well.

"But how did she touch it? Did she touch the same teapot?" Though I've said it, it feels like a weak argument.

"No, Ms. Marple, that's impossible. Reza's lab was closed back then, the poisoned pot was also locked in there and Helena died in the spectroscopy lab, near the diffraction setup."

"Well, let's go then…" I stand up immediately.

"Where to?" Neil is startled.

"To the spectroscopy lab of course! We have loads of Geiger Counters in our department. Let's go and measure the radiation count there, near the diffraction set up," I say, excitedly.

"Hold on, Ms. Marple. This is a police job. The spectroscopy lab is now sealed. We cannot just go in there and break the police seal to enter. I will come back again with the proper paperwork and the police team."

"Won't you take me with you?" I ask anxiously.

"No."

"You are such a bad man!" I exclaim.

"*Paji*?" Neil asks, smiling.

"Exactly," I reply.

"Well, bad luck for you, Ms. Marple, then. Because now you have to go with this *paji* bloke."

"Where to? I have classes now."

I am really surprised. Did not see this coming. Why should I drop everything and go with Neil? And where?

"Forget about your classes. This campus is not safe for you anymore," Neil says calmly.

"What? Why?"

"The murderer or his accomplice must be nearby."

Neil sounds confident. I remember Matt also asked me to be careful yesterday, not to make calls within anyone's earshot. Both seem to be convinced that I am the next target of the killer. But why? Why would they target me?

"How do you know that?" I challenge Neil.

"How did the teapot break, Sri? Right after you measured the radiation level there yesterday afternoon?"

"To get rid of evidence?"

"Precisely. I think we will not get anything from the spectroscopy lab either. Whatever it is that caused Helena's death is no longer there. The murderer got the warning. If only you could have called me without stirring things up yesterday…"

"Amazing, Neil! Now it is my fault, is it? I called you so many times, but you did not pick up. Because you were busy getting scratched by Anthea," I blurt out angrily. A smile briefly appears on Neil's lips but he quickly wipes it away and says, "Hmm. I should have given you my private number. And by the way, the scratching happened much later, in the middle of the night…"

"Spare me the details please!" I cut him short.

"As you wish. I was merely explaining because you asked."

This man really is an arrogant prick. It would be so hard to spend life with this man—what? What am I thinking? Who in their right mind, would like to spend the life with this prick? Not me, for sure. Not in a million years. Why did that stupid thought even come to my mind? Must have been because of all the stress, I am going crazy. I am so happy that he got those painful scratches, he deserves every bit of it. It will make me even happier if Anthea turns out to be a vampire and sucks his blood.

"What are you thinking?" Neil asks again with a hint of a faint smile on his lips.

"If you really think that the murderer is loose then you should order the entire college to be closed for everyone's safety," I comment.

"That is not necessary, I think. They will only target you," says Neil, calmly.

"Jesus! Why? Why only me?"

"Because you started all that commotion yesterday with that blasted teapot. Then you tried calling me. Again, today you rummaged through the garbage with me. Do you think that the murderer or his accomplice did not notice these things?"

"I knew it! You will be the responsible for my downfall. I will fail my exams, and you will be singlehandedly responsible for that," I announce angrily.

"I am fine with that. But I do not wish to be responsible for your death. Come with me," says Neil, as he stood up.

"Where? If you think the college is too risky for me then I can go home," I suggest.

"No. If it is risky here then it will be risky in your home, too. The murderer can follow you there quite easily."

"Then where will I go? I cannot afford a hotel. And I am never going to Aunt Shukla's, no way."

"Who is Aunt Shukla? Sups's friend?"

"Yes. But she is nothing like Suparna, she gossips all the time and is very nosy. I will die anyway if I have to stay with them for more than a day."

"I see! Like my aunts in Kolkata. Alright then, come and stay in my apartment. That's the only option left, I suppose."

"How? You have only one bedroom, where Anthea is now staying," I remind him.

"Anthea? Why? She was there last night, and that's all. Why should she be there every day?" Neil sounds surprised.

"Wow, just for one night?" I cannot help asking.

"I have commitment phobia. Didn't I tell you? Besides, I don't like being scratched on the neck."

"Hmm. Next time observe the size of the nails before fixing the date," I suggest.

"Good point. Your nails are short and nicely clipped though," Neil comments.

"Yeah, actually I bite my nails when I'm stressed, that's why—wait, why are you commenting on my nails?"

"Never mind."

Neil and I leave the restaurant and head to his car. Our first stop is my apartment in Canning Town to gather a few books, clothes, and other essentials. I leave a note for Sadia, letting her know that I was going to Edinburgh with Neil to investigate a case and that she could use my room in my absence. Edinburgh was Neil's suggestion, as he didn't want anyone to know my true whereabouts.

"But Neil, do you suspect even Sadia and Matt?" I ask.

"Before we find the actual murderer, everyone is a suspect, Sri. Besides, even if they are not the murderer, it is a bad idea to tell a secret to many people. 'If more than three people know about it then it is no longer a secret, it is information'." Neil smiles.

"Game of Thrones! Varys." I also smile.

"Indeed! We have got to be careful, Sri. Now switch your phone off and take the SIM out." Neil gives his instructions.

"Why? Oh, I see. Location information? Will they tap my phone?" I ask.

"I don't know if they will, Sri, but they can. So, we have to be careful."

"What if someone calls me?"

"Then they will not reach you," says Neil firmly. "A trifling inconvenience compared to the risk you have otherwise. Don't worry, I will contact Matt and Sadia and cook up a story that you lost your phone or something. It will be believable, you see; your being sloppy might finally pay off!"

We leave the apartment quickly. I cannot help thinking that now it will just be Matt and her in this whole apartment—but forget about it, I can't think about it right now, I have way too many things to worry about already. Anyway, Matt doesn't seem to be even remotely interested in me, he just passes me onto Neil like a hot potato and Neil does the same.

"Tell me one thing, Neil, Reza got killed because he was helping that Iranian ex-spy Nasser Ali to give sensitive documents to journalists. Then why was Helena killed? What is the motive behind her murder?" I ask as we are going to Neil's apartment.

"I don't know, Sri. I am thinking about it, but so far, no luck," Neil confesses.

"Helena's social media accounts?" I ask, thinking of Reza's active social media posts. They always come in handy to understand a person.

"We checked. Nothing there. Helena was not much of a social media person. She only had a Facebook account which she seldom used. Just a few holiday snaps and family photos, that's it," Neil replies.

"Any political affiliation?"

"Nothing. No foreign connection—Iranian, Syrian or Russian… no connection at all. She used to live here alone, in a two-bedroom flat in Camden. Her mother lives in Devon, brother and his family are in Sheffield A few more distant relatives here and there. A very common and rather dull personality."

"Strange! Why should such a boring, middled aged woman be killed by such a sophisticated poison?"

"Yeah. That's why Daniel Morgan, my boss, doesn't think this foreign spy theory has any merit," Neil frowns.

"I see. So, what is his theory then? Why were these two professors killed?"

"Daniels's theory is pretty simple. He thinks it is because of some personal grudges. Reza had a nasty argument with a bunch of yobs in his area recently. They were selling drugs and were threatening elderly people and he stood up to protest."

"You don't normally kill people for an 'argument', do you?" I ask.

"No. And even if you do, it would more likely be stabbing or gunshot at the time, heat of the moment stuff. They wouldn't be plotting such an intricate and sophisticated murder plan using unusual poison." Neil agrees with me.

"Right. And why would they choose his lab as the location? With all these CCTV and swipe cards, it is just asking for danger. Much easier to shot him in an empty park or alley at night," I theorise.

"True."

"What does Daniel say about Helena's murder? Did she also ruffle the feathers of local yobs?" I continue to ask.

"No. But she had some serious trouble with her landlord. They were threatening to sue each other," Neil informed me.

"And the landlord came to poison her in her lab? Doesn't make any sense, Neil."

"Well, that poison thing is still a theory. We could not find or even conclusively say which poison could have been used. The autopsy report doesn't say much either."

I can tell that Neil is playing the devil's advocate to test the strength of our own theory.

"What's your idea, Neil? Why do you think Helena was killed?"

"I think she was collateral damage. She must have heard to seen something which could have been dangerous for the murderer. Anyway, we will talk about it later. Let's go upstairs now."

We have reached Neil's apartment. He parks his car in the basement, and we take the elevator up to his apartment.

Neil asks me to stay in his room and volunteers to sleep on the living room futon again. I don't like to impose like this at all. What kind of threat does he think I am under? Why was he so afraid for my safety? I enter his bedroom, where I stayed just the day before. But last night, Anthea…

"Is everything alright? Do you need anything?" Neil asks me.
"Yeah, alright. But please do me a favour. Could you please change this bedsheet?"
"Why? It's new… Oh, I got it, Anthea. No worries. I will get a fresh one for you. But Sri, now listen to me, carefully. It is serious…"
"What?"
"You must not tell anyone where you are. You must not open the door if I am not here. Not even to any mailman, courier guys, delivery man… to nobody."
"Can I get out if there is a fire in the building?" I joked.
"Yes, you can. But nothing short of that," Neil replies without smiling.
"Neil, how long will this go on? Me, in your room and you on the living room futon. I am feeling really bad, throwing you out of your own room like this."
"Well, that can easily be sorted. If you agree, then we can both stay here. I won't have to take the trouble of sleeping on that hard, uncomfortable futon then." Neil can make the most absurd suggestions with a straight face.

"That's not funny, Neil."

"No, it's not." Neil suddenly looks very, very sombre.

"Sri, I don't know if you are able to understand the gravity of the situation or not, but this is dead serious."

I don't know what to say, so I remain silent.

"Most likely, we are dealing with international terrorism and espionage here. The kind of toxin which killed both of your professors, it must be very, very special. It is not something that a regular contract killer can buy easily from a shoddy backstreet ally. Only a state agency can have access to such sophisticated poison. Like FBI or old KGB. I don't care what my boss Daniel thinks, but it smacks of international terrorism at a very high level." Neil takes a brief pause and then starts again, "The murderer or his accomplice know that you know about the teapot. That you are helping the police to solve the mystery."

"But that's true for you as well. They also know that you are investigating in this case. Are you not in danger too, then?" I remind Neil.

"We are MI6, Sri. This is our job." Neil smiles and then continues, "But I have our whole organization behind me. Every foreign intelligence agency knows that killing an MI6 agent has consequences. But you are just a private individual, an easy target."

What Neil says makes sense. Getting involved into a spy-espionage drama without the protection of a state intelligence agency is dangerous, very, very dangerous.

"But how long will I be in hiding? This can't go on forever."

"I am not sitting idle, Sri, I am working on it. I do have a few hunches. I am trying to confirm them. Give me a couple of days. If I can't do anything by then I will ask our department to arrange formal protection for you. I cannot sleep on that damn futon forever!"

"What do you mean by your 'hunches'?"

"Is it that difficult to understand, Ms. Marple? That teapot incident, how many people know about it?"

"Sadia and Luiza. Also, I took the Geiger from Ed, even though I did not tell him why. But he could have guessed. Are you saying, Neil, that one of them is actually the murderer? No, Neil, they are just students, my friends!"

"I am not saying anything right now, Sri, but anything is possible. What about that professor of yours? Who was present in the condensed matter lab? Did you tell him too?" Neil asks.

"No. He was busy scolding us for not being serious with our experiments. Absolute bollocks—he just doesn't like women scientists. Anyway, we did not tell him anything, just gave him some stupid excuse."

"I see. I don't know who, but one of the people who heard it from you yesterday wanted to destroy the evidence by breaking the teapot and throwing it away. We were just lucky that he missed one broken piece which Natalia threw in the trash, which we finally managed fish out from the garbage."

Lucky indeed! Rummaging through a big wheelie bin full of trash.

"But don't worry too much, just be vigilant. I am also trying my best to nab the murderer. There are fresh bedsheets in that cupboard, help yourself. Goodnight."

Neil goes out, closing the door behind him.

I open the bag that I brought from our apartment and change into pyjamas. Then, as I am changing the bedsheet, a thought suddenly flashes through my mind which makes me freeze.

Apart from my friends and Professor Kowalski, I told another person about the teapot.

Matt!

# *In the Cross-Hairs*

## Alpha Beta Gamma

Next morning, when Neil leaves for work after breakfast, I have nothing to do. Neil's apartment is small, but cozy and functional. He never struck me as a massive interior decoration sort of a guy anyway, but the flat is neat and tidy, not a bachelor's den with unwashed clothes on floor and dirty dished piled up in the sink. The living room features the aforementioned futon and a couple of armchairs, accompanied by a sleek coffee table and a couple of Nordic, minimalist bookshelves that showcase his wide areas of interest; nothing describes a person's personality better than their bookshelf. A large window allows natural light to flood the space and, when open, fills the space with the noise from the streets.

On the other wide, the living room merges with an open plan, compact yet functional kitchen. The kitchen cabinets are painted in a soft grey hue, and the countertops are a polished white quartz. There is a small breakfast bar with a couple of bar stools where Neil and I had our quick breakfast of muesli, fruit, and coffee.

Neil gave me the strict order not to call anyone. So, I can't even call Sadia or Ed or Matt. We told them that I am in Scotland, to help the police in this murder case. Everyone will surely be surprised, but they will possibly believe him nevertheless, because of his official position.

But now the problem is what I should do the whole day? I study for a while, do some complex variable analysis, but I don't have too many books with me. So, I take a shower, remove a Terry Pratchett from Neil's bookshelf, and start reading. Soon I start feeling hungry, so I think about making something nice. But Neil's kitchen looks rather poorly stocked. Just some regular rice, noodles, lentils, and pasta in the cupboard. A pack of Sainsbury's chicken, bacon and sausage in the freezer and a box of withered mushrooms and a very suspicious looking single tomato in the vegetable box. I think of Matt's well stocked kitchen and sighed. Evidently Neil is not a seasoned chef like Matt.

Anyway, I have to make do with whatever is available here. So, I cook rice and chicken curry. Neil does not have all the Indian spices which I would have like to put in there; still, it is edible.

After finishing lunch, I switch on my phone, sans SIM, to login to WhatsApp and send a quick text to Ma and Baba. I hope it should be alright. If I don't contact them today, they will get mighty worried and will start calling Matt or Aunt Shukla or Sadia, creating a lot of chaos.

As I switch the phone off again and started browsing through Neil's bookshelf, the doorbell rings. What should I do? Neil gave very clear instructions. So, I sit tight. The bell rings again. This feels so weird. What am I supposed to do? I tiptoe to the door and peep through the eyehole.

It's Suparna standing outside, with a bag in her hand. As I was thinking whether or not to open the door for her, she rang the bell a third time and started fishing for something from her handbag. She must have the keys with her.

Before she could open the door with her keys, I open the door for her. She was very surprised to see me there.

"Sri! What are you doing here?"
"I, actually I am here since last night…" I start stammering. I don't know what to say without divulging the full details, which I am not allowed to do right now.

Suparna is very surprised for sure. But luckily, she is not as nosy as my aunt Shukla. So hopefully, she is not going to interrogate me. Still, it is a very awkward situation, for sure. I am in my pyjamas. This flat has only one bedroom, the door of which is open. Through that open door the bed is partially visible; my sweater, my scrunchie, the solid-state physics book by Ibach, a notebook, a pen, Robert Galbraith's *The Ink Black Heart*… everything is scattered on that bed. It definitely gives a different vibe, and I cannot tell her the true reason why I am here.

"Did you come to see Neil?" I ask a stupid question (why else should she be here?) to somehow break the ice. "He is not home." I say again.

"I know. We have a spare key to this flat. Still, I rang the doorbell first, just to make sure that I'm not barging into something." Suparna smiles. "Honestly, I did not expect to find YOU here! But I am happy, very happy," her smile widens.

"No, no. It's not what it looks like. We are just—" I start to protest.

"I know! I am not putting any pressure on you, Sri. You two have just met. Take your time to get to know each other well. No rush!" Another sweet smile.

It is not helping, not helping at all. She thinks we are dating and whatever I am trying to say is only bolstering her notion about our relationship.

"But Sri, your college is open today, is it not?"

"Yes, it is. But actually—" I am thinking hard to come up with a believable excuse for bunking college to be here in Neil's apartment mid-afternoon.

"I know why!" Suparna smiles mysteriously.

(What does she know? Did Neil tell her anything? About our case?)

"Basically, you want to spend his birthday together, isn't it?" Suparna spills it out at last.

(Really? Is this his birthday, too, today?)

"That's reasonable. But don't bunk your classes every day like this, Sri!" Suparna cautions me. "Do you know when Neil will be back?"

"I don't know."

(Finally, a truthful answer.)

"I bet he will be back soon. He won't keep you waiting for long." Suparna says confidently.

"Not sure. He is rather busy with a case," I reply.

"Regarding those deaths at your college, right?"

I am a bit surprised. Does Neil talk about his cases with his family, in detail? He was thrifty with information to me at least! Perhaps Suparna understands my train of thought, as she says, "Obviously, Neil doesn't talk about all his cases with everyone. But I know a bit about this one because he asked for my help." Suparna explains.

"Your help? Why?"

"He asked me to hack a few Tor communications. He thinks those communications may help to get to the murderer."

"Tor communication?"

"Yes, perhaps you know it. Tor is a highly secure browser. It is practically impossible to eavesdrop there. That's why it is very popular among spies all over the world to communicate securely with their friends."

"Interesting! But doesn't MI6 have its own hacking team?"

"Yes. But Neil's boss does not want to involve them."

"Yes, I know. Daniel thinks that Neil is unnecessarily complicating things."

"Exactly. That is why Neil is seeking unofficial helps. A bit from me. A bit from another girl in their department— Mirella, she is in message deciphering. Purely as a personal favour. Neil and Mirella are good friends."

Of course! Neil is so popular among ladies. Once again Suparna seems to have read my mind. "What I mean is they are just friends. Please don't think otherwise, Sri." Suparna quickly wants to clarify herself.

"No, why should I think that? But this Tor communication, could you hack it?"

"Not yet. It is very difficult, Sri. Their network has more than seven thousand proxies. It is virtually impossible to identify any network packet there. That's why I am trying to tap a client machine before it enters Tor. But no success so far, I am afraid."

"I see."

"Anyway, I must leave now."

"Why? So soon? Stay for a little longer, Neil will be back. Would you like to have some tea?"

"No, Sri, not now. I am in a hurry today. Tell Neil that I came and give this to him." She takes a lunchbox out of her bag and gives it to me.

"I am not a great cook, but I made *kheer* (a sort of rice pudding) for him. Aniket wants to do it for him on this birthday, so I do it for him every year. I did not know that you will be here too, otherwise I would have made some more. But never mind, share it together."

"OK. But I need to ask you for a favour, Suparna…"

"Yes, what is it?"

"Don't tell anyone that I am staying here. I mean definitely not to Aunt Shukla or anybody else."

"Don't worry, I am not that close to Shukla." Suparna smiles and then continues, "She is very nosy. She was already telling people in her friend circle that you have bagged a boyfriend and are spending nights with him. I protested; said what is the big deal? It is only natural for a single girl of your age. But then she turned on me saying I have no moral scruples because I married a divorced man. Forget about them."

I remain silent. Suparna continues, "You stayed here a couple of days back, too, right? That's the boyfriend Shukla was talking about, isn't it?"

"Y-yeah… I mean…"

"That's fine. You don't need to explain anything to me. I told you; I am happy. Aniket was feeling a bit sad that Neil will be spending his birthday alone. I will tell him not to worry; Neil now has company."

Jesus! This is impossible. How long will this play acting go on? I sit on the futon and start thinking after Suparna leaves. This futon is really hard, must be difficult to sleep here. I can't even go to the balcony. So, I stand behind the curtain and look outside through the window. I can see roads from here. It is past two thirty now. A bunch of kids are returning from school. And then I see a man… It's Neil… he is coming towards this building.

But he is not alone. There is a girl with him. Is she his new date? Birthday special? Oh God, what should I do now? Will he bring her to this apartment? Where will I go then?

But no, they stop in front of the gate, chat for a while and then Neil hails a black cab… the girl is getting into the cab. Neil kisses her on both cheeks and bids her goodbye. Good heavens! The girl is so young, probably not even twenty, ginger, with blue eyes and a face full of freckles. Does he really go out with girls this young?

The cab drives off and Neil enters the building. I move away from the window.

I know what's going on here. This is another casual date of Mr. Neil Basu. To celebrate his birthday. Could not bring her inside because I am staying here. That means he did not go to the office today. I am stuck here like a prisoner and there he is, in no hurry to nab the murderer. He just doesn't have time to chase criminals. Too busy fixing a new date every other day, a real-life James Bond.

Such a young girl, he should be ashamed of himself. Let him come upstairs. I will confront him. This cannot go on. I don't care if criminals are targeting me or not, I can't spend days like this, in house arrest.

In a short while, Neil entered the apartment using his own key.

"I want to go home." I blurt out as soon as Neil enters.

"What happened, Ms. Marple?" Neil seems surprised.

"I don't want to stay. It's so inconvenient for you…"

"Yeah, sleeping on this blasted futon is inconvenient, but what to do? On the other hand, you're at risk. So…"

"No risk. Matt will be there in my apartment. He can help me."

"And what if your handsome flatmate is the murderer?"

"What do you mean?" I frowned.

"You told him about the teapot. Didn't you? What is this?"
Neil pointed towards the lunchbox containing kheer. "Did Sups come here?" asks Neil after opening the box.

"Yes, she came and left this for you, for your birthday."

"Sups does this every year." Neil smiles happily.

"Yeah, she told me. Happy Birthday. But Matt is not the murderer."

"Thanks. How do you know that Matt is not the murderer?"

"I just know," I say stubbornly.

"Well, this is not really like Ms. Marple. You have no evidence to prove his innocence."

"Do you have any evidence of him being guilty?" I ask.

"Not yet. But I am trying …"

"Yeah, right!" I roll my eyes.

"What is that eyeroll supposed to mean, Sri?"

"I mean you have no time to work on this case. You have other priorities."

"Other priorities? Like what?"

"Like this morning. When you went to look for a young date, to celebrate your birthday…"

"A date? In the morning? Where would I find someone?"

"How do I know where do you get your partners from? Look, I don't want to be judgmental, but you should really not go out with a girl this young. How old are you?"

"Turned twenty-eight today. But which girl? What are you blabbering about? You are the only girl in my life right now, and that in a strictly platonic way."

"Then who was that girl who went in the taxi? Your grandma?"

"No. My sister."

"W-What?"

"Lucy. My half-sister. She came from Glasgow."

"H-How come? She is ginger, blue eyes, freckles, no Indian features at all…"

"Both her parents are Scottish, whereas I am mixed. That's why. We have different fathers, but still, she is my baby sister, my only sibling. She came here to spend my birthday together. But I had to send her away because you are staying here and there is no room."

"I-I am so sorry. Where will she stay?"

"With my dad and Sups."

"But… they are not—"

"No, they are not related to Lucy. But we have a blended family. I know it looks strange to you, but it works for us."

"I am really sorry, Neil." I apologize after a pause.

"Yes, you should be. How could you think that I will go out with an eighteen-year-old? It's sick!"

"Sorry. How would I know what kinds of girls you like—"

"True. You have absolutely no idea about that."

"What do you mean?"

"Nothing. Would you like to have some kheer?"

"Yes. But you first. The birthday boy! I would have arranged a gift had I known earlier."

"I just want one gift from you. Don't harp on going back and make it easier for the murderer."

As Neil goes to the bathroom, I pour the kheer in a nice bowl and go looking for a candle.

"Did you make any progress on the case?" I ask Neil when he comes back.

"Not much. But you should know a few things. Do you know why I didn't pick up your call that day?"

"Yes, I know. Because of that Anthea—"

"Jesus! I met Anthea the night before, we spent a night together, end of story."

"I see. If she didn't scratch your neck, would you go out with her again?"

"God, I can't believe I am having this conversation. Listen, she does not have my work phone number—"

"Do you frequently pick up girls at bars like this?"

"Jesus fucking Christ! I did not pick anyone up. It was a consensual and casual agreement."

"How frequently do you get into such consensual casual relations?"

"Don't know. I don't keep a logbook. Look, it is pretty normal here. Don't girls come over to Matt?"

"Yes. A lot. He doesn't keep any logbook either."

"Look Sri, I told you before. My life experience is way more than yours. A twenty-three-year-old virgin like you is not very common here."

"Twenty-four-year-old."

"What?"

"It is my birthday, too."

"Seriously?"

"Yep. There are eight billion people in this world and just 365 days in a year. You do the math," I say coolly.

"I see! So how did you spend your birthday?"

"What could I do? You have forbidden everything. For you, your sister came, stepmum brought kheer…"

"I told you I'll share the kheer with you, didn't I? No need to be so dramatic."

"The kheer is not the main point, Neil. I could not even speak to my parents over the phone. Just sent a WhatsApp message a little while back, that's it."

"What? What did you say, Sri? WhatsApp message? Did you switch your phone on?" Neil sounded alarmed.

"Neil, they would be worried like hell if I didn't even drop a text message to them on my birthday."

"Well, they will have a much bigger reason to be worried now. You could have used my phone, or Sup's phone to call, if you were that desperate. I did not expect this from you, Sri. You should have been a lot more careful." Neil sounds worried and vexed at the same time.

"What's the big deal, Neil?"

"A lot, Sri. I told you that you are on the radar of an international spy network. They think you know too much. Now you have divulged your location. When they see that you are staying with me, they will get even more alarmed."

I remain silent. Neil speaks again after a pause.

"Take a few essentials in a small bag, I'll do the same. Then let's go."

"Go? Where to?"

"Don't know. We have to improvise. Let's get out of here now."

"Have a spoonful of kheer first…"

"No time for that, Sri. When did you send the WhatsApp?"

We are talking while stuffing a few essentials in our bags. Things like chargers, toothbrush, a change of clothes, comb etc.

"Maybe half an hour or forty-five minutes back? A little before Suparna came." I reply, as I zip my bag up.

"Then it is already late. This flat is no longer safe for us. I hope we will at least have the time to get out of this building before they come." says Neil as he tied his shoelaces.

Then he calls the lobby manager downstairs and tells him that we are going out to celebrate his birthday. If any guest come looking for us, he should give him the message.

Just before we got out of the flat, through the window, we see a black car parking in front of the building.

\*\*\*

Neil and I do not take the elevator down from his flat but take the stairs instead. After getting down to the ground floor, we get out through the fire escape door which leads us straight to a back street. This is the back of the apartment building. The black car which we saw from the window is parked at the front, on the main road.

This is really a deserted back street alley, not many people around. The street ends in a T-junction in about three hundred meters from here. Cars are parked on both sides of this street. We have to go to the main road to get any bus, taxi, or tube. There are terraced houses on the left-hand side of the street and, on the right, there is a big park with one of its small side gates leading to this street.

As we start walking towards the main street, we see someone coming from the opposite direction. It is already quite dusky on this November London day. Neil grabs my arm and drags me inside the park through the small side gate.

"Kiss me, Sri," I hear him whispering.

"What?!" I almost shout out loud.

But Neil pulls me towards him before I could finish my sentence.

"Do as I say," he whispered again.

Before I can react, I can feel his lips pressing against mine. He keeps on pressing them until my lips open, I can feel his tongue, his right hand is around my waist, his left hand pulls the scrunchie out of my ponytail to let my hair spread around my face and shoulders.

I could not say how long we stood like this, it felt like an eternity. In reality though, it must have been less than a couple of minutes.

"I think he is gone." Neil speaks in a normal voice as he wipes his wet lips with the back of his palm.

"What the hell was that?" I shout as I push him hard.

"Didn't you say that you only get into consensual liaisons? When did I ever give you my consent?" I am seething with rage.

"Stop it, Sri! Stop behaving like a child." Neil speaks in a hushed but serious tone. "Whether you like it or not, you are in the middle of a spy thriller now. So, act like one. Stop this nonsense of Victorian prudery and think of saving your life… and mine."

"What do you mean?"

"That man in the alley, most likely he came in that black car. Since they couldn't find us in our apartment, he came down to survey the neighbourhood. People usually don't look at the kissing couple in a park. Even if they do, they cannot see the faces very clearly. I even spread your hair out to hide your face better."

Now I understand. At the same, I time feel bad for misunderstanding Neil's motives.

"If you keep on thinking that I want to take advantage of you, then we are indeed in serious trouble. You have got to trust me, Sri. You have no other option. Now let's go."

"Did they go?" I finally ask.

"Possibly. But they may come back again in the night, when we are back from 'celebrating my birthday'!" Neil smiles bitterly.

We come out through the other side of the park. First, we take a black cab to Paddington. From there we take a bus to Baker Street. Then we take the underground to Kings Cross station. I suppose Neil was intentionally taking a convoluted route to make it difficult for 'them' to track or follow us.

When we arrived at King's Cross, I thought we might take a train from there, but Neil rented a car from Hertz instead. After completing the formalities at the car rental, we got the keys, grabbed a sandwich each and Neil started driving as I sat on the passenger seat.

"Where are we going, Neil?" I ask.
"Royston." he replies.
"And where is that?"
"A little before Cambridge, a small town."
"Why are we going there?"

"As good as anywhere else," Neil shrugs. "We need a place to stay low for some time. A small, sleepy village should be fine for that," he explains further.

"Do we really need to take all this trouble?"

But before he can answer, Neil's phone starts ringing. He answers the call and speaks for a minute or two. When he finishes the call, his face is very serious.

"Who was it? Your dad?" I thought so, listening to the one side of the conversation.

"Yes. Dad and Sups took Lucy out for dinner. When they came back, they found the house had been burgled."

"My God!"

"The burglars came through the patio door. Ransacked the house but nothing was stolen, it seems."

"Were they just ordinary burglars, Neil?"

"Don't think so. Thank heavens that Lucy was there. Otherwise, dad and Sups would have been at home. Can you imagine, Sri, what these reckless people would have done to them? They are professional killers, for God's sake." says Neil in a very anxious tone.

"Did they come for me?" I finally ask as my throat feels dry.

"I would think so. They already know that I kept you in my flat. Since we fled that place, they took their chance to look at dad's house as well." Neil reasons.

I begin to feel really bad now. I should have been more careful with my phone. I am exposing a lot of people to danger by my reckless behaviour.

"I am so sorry, Neil. It's all my fault. I didn't think it would be so dangerous. Since you asked last night, I took the SIM out of my phone. I just switched it on a for a few minutes, sans the SIM, just connected to your home wi-fi and used the WhatsApp. That's all." I try to explain myself. I really thought it would be safe. But apparently, it is not.

"Sri, you should know better. You know the basics of cyber security, don't you? The phones these days are a nuisance. As soon as you switch them on, all those apps start accessing your location information."

"But I do not give location access to my apps. I mean not by default. I only give permission when I absolutely need it, for example when I use Google Maps. And I only ever grant temporary, in-the-app access, never always on access."

"That's a good strategy, Sri. But WhatsApp itself is not the most secure messaging application, I am afraid," Neil comments.

"Why do you say that? Doesn't it have end to end encryption?" I ask.

"So what? Only the text message body is encrypted, not the metadata. They will not be able to read your message text, but from the metadata they can find your IP address or location. That is fairly simple, at least for professional hackers."

Neil is right. I should have thought about this possibility. After all we are dealing with a very efficient and shrewd foreign agency here, not amateur people.

"You are right. I need to be more careful in the future. Seems I need to change a lot…"

"Or just change your messaging app. Don't use WhatsApp. Use Signal. Signal uses sealed sender technique. It encrypts even the metadata," Neil smiles.

"Hmm. Good suggestion. But tell me one thing Neil, did you know that they are watching us? I mean before today?"

"That's what I was going to tell you yesterday. But you diverted the discussion with your silly Anthea questions. These people, they bugged my phone. That's why I had to erase all the data from my previous work phone and get them re-installed on my new phone. That is the reason my work phone was off for a such a long time. Otherwise, I always keep it with me, even in bed."

"I see!" I think for a while in silence and then ask the weird question that has been bothering me for a while now. "What if, an urgent call comes during… I mean …when you are in the middle of, you know …"

"In the middle of sex? Why? Haven't you seen the Bond movies? How he keeps his gun under his pillow and then shoots three guys with one shot and then escapes dangling from the helicopter?"

"Do they teach you these things in your training?"

"Of course! They also give us Bond girls to practice with. Come now, we have reached our destination."

Neil stops the car in front of a medium sized old, Victorian house with a big garden. The neighbourhood seems sleepy, a few lamps on the street were lit dimly, which did nothing to reduce the darkness. Neil parks the car in the nearby car park and switches off the engine.

"Who lives here?" I ask.

"This is a bed and breakfast. Let's go inside." Neil replies.

I adjust my glasses over my (flattish) nose and observe carefully. There was a sign above the front door at a distance, which sways gently in the wind, creaking softly. It reads The Ivy Manor. As I take my bag and start moving, he speaks again, "By the way, I have not booked it in our real names. So just keep mum and let me handle it. Is that clear?"

"Aye-aye, Sir!" I mock a salute.

"Oh my! That's an awful accent, Sri! I will teach you the correct way of saying it. I am half Scottish, after all. Now let us go."

We walk into a smallish lobby where a kindly woman with silver hair and a pink cardigan greets us with a smile. Neil gives his booking information, shows his (fake) ID and gets the keys. Following the direction of the receptionist, we go up a narrow staircase that creaks with each step.

"Why did you book just one room?" I ask as we walk through the corridors.

"Why would Mr. and Mrs. Gonzales stay in different rooms?" Neil asked back.

"Why did you make me Mrs. Gonzales?"

"Otherwise, they would have asked for your ID, too. Do you have any fake ID, Ms. Marple?"

"But this Gonzales…"

"One of my aliases. Our department made it for me."

"Wow! Is this the only one? Or do you have more?" I am fascinated.

"I have a few more. Each one of us investigators have a few. It helps us doing our jobs."

"Wicked! Can you tell me what your other aliases are?"

"No. I can't tell you that."

"Why? Can't you tell the missus?"

"It is forbidden to tell even the real missus. The fake missus is out of question!"

"I see! Do you use these aliases to pick the girls up from bars?" I am curious.

"God! What do you mean by 'picking up girls'? I do not pick anyone up from anywhere. I told you it's consensual—"

"Yes, yes, I know. I am asking about those consensual-casual pickups."

"Look, no one can be a James Bond if they have a to give their character certificates all the time."

"Hmm, so it's not license to kill, it is actually license to—"

"Don't even think about finishing that sentence!"

Entering into our room, I find that the arrangement is not too bad. It is a large room with two single beds in the two corners. If only there were a divider wall, it would have been the same arrangement as Neil's flat. Neil is observing my reaction. Now he asks, "Will this do, Ms. Marple?"

"Yes, it will. Thanks!"

It has been a really long day with a lot of mental stress. I can feel the adrenaline going down, leaving me exhausted. I think of going to bed straight, but suddenly a thought comes to my mind. "Neil, that number, I mean the one that Reza wrote before dying…"

"Yes, what about it?"

"I was thinking, 210-138. Could it be related to any element in the periodic table?"

"Which element, Sri? If we assume 210 is the mass number but what is 138, then? It cannot be any atomic number. There just 111 elements in the periodic table. How can 138 be the atomic number of any element?"

"Perhaps it is not the atomic number then?"

"Then what is it? Normally elements are identified by their mass number and atomic number, and they are given together to uniquely identify an element, isn't it?"

"But 210 is probably an isotope of polonium. Is it not?" I enquired.

"Most likely. It has about 40 isotopes, 210 is probably one of them. But Polonium's atomic number is 84. Also, remember that we did not detect any gamma radiation in the Geiger. Even within the teapot, the level was not fatal. The theory doesn't stand up as it is, I am afraid." Neil says in a dark voice.

"Hmm, you are right. Perhaps we are missing something. Anyway, let's call it a day now. To be frank, this is probably the worst birthday ever, for both of us. What do you think?" I smile.

"Not for me. That was my 8th. Birthday." Neil smiles back.

"Worse than this? What happened?"

"My parents' divorce got finalized that day."

"Oh! I am sorry. But I thought you are happy in your blended family…"

"Yeah, my family is nice. I am happy that both mum and dad are happy with their new partners instead of being miserable together. Both Kevin and Sups are nice people. I love Lucy to bits…"

"…But?"

"But that was a tough time, Sri, I won't lie. An eight-year-old boy doesn't understand all these relationship complications. That's why, I think, people got to be very, very careful before committing to a long-term relationship. It is too damn risky, in my opinion. I will never be able to take such a risk."

"Of course! You are just an MI6 investigator. What do you know of risk!"

"It's different kind of risk, Sri! It's much better to—"

"—To keep doing the consensual casual. Happy Birthday, Neil."

I hold a paper out towards him. I just drew a pencil sketch on the writing pad of this B&B and have folded it like a card.

"Cool! You're a really good artist, Sri!" Neil sounds happy. "But what should I give you—?"

I come over, bend my face towards him and he pecks a kiss lightly on my cheeks.

"Happy birthday, Sri! Stay as you are, don't change a bit… ever."

Neil's phone rings before he could finish wishing me happy birthday. He takes the call and speaks for about a minute. His face grows very dark.

"My God!" He sits on the edge of the bed, holding his head in his two hands.

I become alarmed and ask, "What happened, Neil?"

"It was the lobby manager from my apartment. My neighbours heard some strange noise coming from my flat and they alerted them."

"Did you get burgled, too?"

"They opened the flat with their master key and found a dead cat under the dining table."

"A dead cat?" I am sad and surprised at the same time.

"Yes, the neighbour's cat, Lorna. She used to come to my flat occasionally through the balcony. In fact, the noise was from that cat, the poor thing was crying in agony before dying."

"Why Neil? How did the cat die?"

"She ate the kheer! We left in on the table, on a bowl, uncovered... remember?" Neil sounds grave.

"Oh my god! But how is that possible Neil? Suparna bought that kheer, didn't she?"

Neil does not say anything, just sits there fixing his gaze on the floor. He finally lifts his head after a minute and asks, "Who bugged my phone, Sri? The foreign spies or someone closer to home?" Neil whispers. He is looking pathetic. I have no answer for him.

Neil buries his face in his palms again and whispers in a muffled voice, "I don't know who to trust anymore!"

## *On the Run*

"Good morning, Sri!"

It takes me a while to remember where I am. I have been waking up in a different place every morning for the last few days now. No wonder I am feeling a little confused. I take my glasses from the bedside table, put them on and look at Neil. He looks fresh, showered and all set for the day.

"Morning! Is it late?" I ask.

"A bit. It's almost nine. Now get ready fast. They only serve breakfast until nine thirty."

Neil is looking much better now after that dangerous rumination last night. Showered and shaven, he is looking all fresh now.

"You are looking better today, Neil."

"Yep. I gave it some thought, you see. The point is, I don't have enough proof to suspect Sups. So, I decided to keep this evil stepmother theory on hold for now. The *kheer* could also have been poisoned later, after we left the flat. Who knows, perhaps they got into to the apartment after we left and poisoned it, thinking we would have it after coming back."

"True. But it is a detective's job to suspect everyone." I remind Neil.

"No, Sri, a detective's job is not to suspect everyone. Their job is to do the logical analysis based on the available facts and data. And the logic says Sups has known me for more than ten years now. She is not my mum, but she is family. She had always been very nice to me. Should I ignore all these facts and make her Snow White's evil stepmother based on a flimsy speculation?"

Neil had a point and I had to admire him to be able to do such cool-headed calculation amidst such rampant killings and conspiracies.

"Fair enough. Don't do that. But then I should also follow the same rule?" I proclaim.

"What do you mean?"

"I mean Matt. We do not have any conclusive proof against Matt either. So, I will also give him the benefit of doubt," I firmly declare.

"I see! It seems you can't keep your handsome flatmate in your bad books for long. And yet, I am the one who is getting blamed for the romantic liaisons!" Neil feigns frustration.

"I told you not to push me to Matt like a hot potato."

"When did I ever do that? I am trying just the opposite. That kiss in the park yesterday, seems it had no effect whatsoever on you. My confidence is shaken, Sri!"

"Wasn't that supposed to be only for saving our lives?"

"It was. But let's say you throw some wood into the fire to save your life. But even then, the wood should burn and flare up the fire. Otherwise, you might think that the wood was damp."

"That's the worst innuendo I've ever heard, Neil. Now let's go and have breakfast before it finishes."

Just before leaving the room Neil reminds me, "Don't call me Neil in front of the others."

"What should I call you, then? Laal?"

"Laal? Why? Doesn't that mean red in Bengali?"

"Yes. Just as Neel means blue in Bengali." I explain.

"Oh, that way! No, neither Laal, nor Neel. My alias is now Antony Gonzales. So, call me Tony."

"Antony Gonzales? Seriously?"

I can't help thinking of the famous Bollywood movie character from the seventies with the same name.

"Yes. So what?" Clearly, Neil is not aware of the reference.

"You don't watch much Bollywood movie, do you?"

"None at all. Why?"

"Well, after all this is over, I will take you to a famous one and then you will understand the Antony Gonzales reference. I am a penniless pauper, but still, this one will be on me." I promise.

"Very well, I will look forward to that. By the way, Matt could not reach you, so he wished you happy birthday through me. Here it is."

Neil shows a birthday e-card on his mobile. Nice rose petals drop as soon as he clicks on the e-card. It is followed by a recorded video message from Matt and Sadia together. They recorded it from our living room sofa.

"They will make a cute couple." I comment, as I returned the phone to Neil.

"Who?" Neil clearly can't follow my train of thought.

"Matt and Sadia." I clarify.

"Jesus! You are so jealous, Sri!" Neil exclaims.

"Nothing to be jealous of, Neil. Matt is not my boyfriend. He can date whomever he fancies." I reply in a matter-of-fact way.

"Your psychology needs studying, Sri. You are not with Matt, yet you can't stand Sadia near him. You are not with me either, yet you are jealous of Anthea. Do you get jealous only for jealousy's sake?"

"I am not jealous of anyone, Neil. Just that I don't get this casual sex, this constant parade of women, devoid of any mental or intellectual connection… I really don't get it. Don't you guys feel tired?"

"Do you know who do you sound like? Like your Aunt Shukla. Why were you so upset when she judged you? Why did you take your anger out on your own mum then?"

It is my fault, really. I should never have given those details to Neil.

"I told you already, this is how it works here, at least in our age group. Me or Matt, none of us are medieval monks. We have our needs; we want to explore the options before settling down… if we want to settle down at all, that is. Everybody does it here. So, my suggestion to you would be, when in Rome do as Romans do." Neil concludes his speech.

I am not sure I liked his advice very much, but I don't want to argue any further. It is pointless, really. We have different outlooks and different expectations from life. Which is fine, everyone does not have to be the same, the world will be pretty dull that way. Moreover, we are being chased by some notorious and reckless gang of people. We have bigger things to worry about than dating protocols.

"Come, Sri. Let me take you somewhere." Said Neil after finishing the breakfast.

"Where to?"

"You will see. Come now."

"But—"

"Why worry? We do not have much to do here anyway. We can't even browse through our phones. Being locked up the whole day in a room like this, it is simply awful. Would have been different if I had a girl with me, though!"

"I AM a girl, Neil!"

"Nah, you are just Sri."

"What is that supposed to mean?"

I am wondering whether to feel insulted or not.

"It means we are comrades now, allies. Our genders are irrelevant." Neil explains.

"What a relief. Let's go then, wherever you want to take me to…"

Neil does not take the car. He said the place is really close by and we can just walk. The town is small and charming and, as we started walking, we pass by a few nice, little shops and cafes. One shop catches my eyes with its display of vintage books, and I make a mental note to return and explore it later.

We go past the empty market square and continue to walk through the picturesque alleys, adorned with nice little houses with their neatly maintained hedges and front garden still displaying a few late bloomers. I can see that we were walking towards the fields, away from the village centre. Finally, we stop in front of a lovely, two storey white house with honeysuckle adorning the porch. This is the last house in the street, next to it is the wide-open undulating fields displaying the quintessential beauty of the English countryside. We can hear the small stream flowing by the back garden. Very pretty indeed, almost from a children's book, though I am yet to understand the significance of this house. Surely Neil didn't bring me here just because it is pretty!

"Whose house is this, Neil?"

"Not sure whose is it now, but it used to be ours." He gives a rueful smile.

"Really?" I am surprised.

"Yes. We used to live here when I was little, mum, dad, and me. Dad used to work in the hospital. Do you see that red-brick house over there, in the corner? It used to be my nursery school." Neil points towards the house at the beginning of the street.

"Happy childhood memories?" I smile.

"Indeed. And then, some unhappy ones, but that's life," says Neil after a pause.

I remain silent. Neil goes on with his reminiscence, almost like a soliloquy, "Dad met mum when he was still a student of medicine in Edinburgh. Mum was a waitress at a local restaurant. She was stunning."

"That's not hard to believe, looking at you!"

Neil pays no attention to my compliment, but keeps on saying, "But their backgrounds were different, culturally, intellectually. Maybe that's why it didn't work out. Now both are happy with people closer to their backgrounds." He shrugs with a smile.

"I think you are missing an important point here though, Neil."

"What is that?"

"Love! The great equalizer."

"Blimey, Sri! No one over the age of twelve believe in that tosh!"

I can see what's bothering Neil. No matter what he says, that poisoned *kheer* was still tormenting him—a lot. That is the reason behind all these cynical reminiscences.

In a way I see his point, but I still have a hard time picturing Suparna as a murderer. I just don't buy this theory of the evil stepmother. It doesn't make any sense. Suparna never seemed like a dumb person to me. So, trying to poison Neil like this when there are witnesses who can vouch that the dessert came from her, and the lunchbox will bear her fingerprints all over it… no, it would be suicide for her. Most importantly, the motive. What motive does she have to do something this drastic? I honestly thought she liked Neil and even if she didn't, she had loads of opportunities in the past ten years. But I can also empathize with Neil's anxiety.

"Which one was your room?" I want to change the subject.

"That one, upstairs, on the left. The one on the right was mum and dad's. Mum used to sing a song every night while tucking me in, she has beautiful voice; now what was it… let me remember… something to do with doon… and banks…"

"Scottish song? Folk?" I think I know which one he means.

"Yes. *Ye banks and braes o holy doon*… and then… I can't remember… it was ages ago."

"*How can ye bloom sae fresh an fair…*" I add.

"Yes, that's right, absolutely! How do you know that?" Neil is genuinely surprised.

But before I can answer his question, Neil drags me behind the thick hedges of the house next door. For a moment, I am half expecting a repeat performance of the park yesterday, but nothing like that happens. Soon, a silver car drives past, but the driver looks like a normal bloke to me; a bit stocky built, but that's about it. Can't see any weapon or any other suspicious thing either. But Neil's facial expression has changed completely.

"Any problem, Neil?" I whisper.
"Yes, a big one. We have to go." Neil whispers back.
"Where? To the hotel?"
"No. Not to the hotel. That location is now compromised."
"What do you mean?"
"I mean we have to leave Royston, Sri. Now." Neil sounds grave.
"How?"
"We can go through those fields… to the train station. Not very far, six, seven minutes' walk, max. I know the way." He has already started walking that way, as he speaks.
"But… our stuff, the rented car?"
"We have to leave them all, I am afraid. You have your phone and your purse with you, don't you?"
I nod affirmatively.

"But Neil, why? What happened suddenly?" I ask as we started walking through the fields.

"I will tell you, Sri, soon. Now, let's hurry."

We reach the station in seven minutes. Thankfully, there is a train towards Cambridge in nine minutes. We get the tickets and board it. As the train starts moving, Neil finally relaxes a bit.

"Where are we going, Neil?"

"Where this train goes. To Cambridge."

"Shall we stay there? In Cambridge?"

"No. We will rent another car from there."

"Then, where will we go from there?"

"I don't really know. Do you happen to know any good place close to Cambridge?"

"What does that mean? Are you not sure where we are going?"

"Nope, not at all. You saw the whole thing, Sri. Does it look pre-planned? Does any of it remotely looked planned? I am improvising as we go."

"But why are we on the run? Why are we moving from place to place under aliases like fugitives?"

"Wait a little longer, Sri, just a little longer. Perhaps you realize that I have something to tell you. But not here, not in this public place. Let us wait till we check in to our hotel room."

"'Our' room? Is this a permanent thing now? This Mr. and Mrs. Gonzales, will this go on forever?"

"Nothing goes on forever in this universe, Sri. Even the stars die. People who seek eternal love tend to forget that," says Neil, looking at the fields outside the train window.

"That's the biggest hyperbole I have ever heard."

"Possibly! Anyways, the day of Gonzales is now over. Enter the Shettys."

"Another alias? Why?"

"I don't like the same thing for long. You know that, right?"

"Of course, I do. Like Anthea, your queen for only one night."

"True."

We get down at Cambridge and Neil goes straight to a car rental place again. After renting the car, first we go to a shopping mall to buy some bare essentials. Then the journey starts again. I still don't know where we are going. Hopefully Neil knows, because he is driving.

"No questions. No questions at all." I mumble in Bengali.

"What did you say?" Neil is startled.

"Nothing!" I reply.

"Why do you do it, Sri? You know that I don't know that language. Do you want to make fun of me?"

"Don't you think, any source of fun in these circumstances should be treasured?"

"You're right! Carry on then. Entertain yourself. Keep speaking in Bengali."

"Neil, have you ever thought how the number of Bengalis are increasing in your life?"

"What do you mean? Obviously, my dad's relatives—"

"I am not talking about them, Neil; they are far away. If you look closer home, first Suparna…"

"Yes, but she has been around for quite some time now. Hardly a recent addition."

"True. But I am quite a recent addition."

"Are you an addition to my life, Sri?"

"Why not? We have already spent three nights together. According to some ancient Sanskrit wisdom, you become friends if you take seven steps together. We have taken way more steps together than that, didn't we? Now we are running up and down the country to save our lives. Would you say our lives are not joined like Siamese twins?"

"Are you trying to hit on me, Sri?" Neil smiles as he momentarily takes his eyes off the road to glance at me.

"What would you do, if I did?"

"Sweetheart, I am always up for consensual-casual… and you know that."

"But I am not."

"And I know that." Neil gives a charming smile.

"Right. So, nothing can ever happen between us. Never." I say confidently.

"Never say never, sweetheart." Neil smiles again and keeps driving.

After a little while he asks me again, "I didn't get to ask you back then. How did you learn that Scottish folk song? That Banks and Braes? Have you ever been to Scotland?"

"No, I have never been there. But Tagore had been there."

"Tagore? The poet?" Neil seems very surprised.

"Yes, the poet. And the songwriter. He liked that tune and created a Bengali composition to the same tune."

"Really? I never knew that!"

"Yes Neil. Cultures are often much more closely related than they seem to. We human beings are not that different from each other, you know."

"Yes, you are right. We share ninety-nine percent of our genes with chimps; so whatever variations we see among ourselves are within that last one percent. Here… we have arrived Sri."

Neil parks the car under the porch of a lovely old Victorian building with a hoarding that reads, "Nags Head Bed and Breakfast, Grantchester."

\*\*\*

After we enter the designated room for Mr. and Mrs. Shetty, I sit on the big armchair and ask.

"So …?"

"Yes, Sri, you deserve some explanation." Neil sits on the smaller chair.

"Right. For example, you suspect there is a mole in your department. Someone pretty high up."

"You are clever, Sri!"

"You don't have to be too clever to deduce this, Neil, do you? The way you are running around with me, if everything were alright, then MI6 itself could have given me protection. Or asked the Met police to do so. Isn't it?"

This suspicion has been in my mind since London. Especially after dramatically leaving Neil's flat yesterday. Why didn't Neil call his boss or colleagues or somebody else in the police? Why did he have to take all the risk personally, take all the burden? It never felt like he told anyone in his office that we were in Royston.

"Yes, Sri. My suspicion started growing after a few incidents. I think our department is compromised. I mean not everyone, obviously, but someone is working as a double agent. That person is supplying the crucial information to our enemies, trying to erase evidence."

"Did you start to suspect this after your phone got bugged?"

"That's of course one of the things that got me suspecting. Another fishy thing is this whole attempt to paint this as a case of thallium poisoning."

"Even if it is thallium Neil, who gave it to Reza? What does Mr. Daniel Morgan say about that?"

"Well, Daniel has his theory. Those yobs in Reza's locality, some of them are drug peddlers. Reza got into some arguments with them."

"Yes, you mentioned that before. What happened there, exactly?"

"There is this gang of boys in Reza's locality. The leader is a guy called Ben. They had a few convictions and accusations of some petty thefts, shoplifting, mugging etc."

"I think that is common in every locality in every big city, Neil. What has Reza got to go with that? Was he trying to reform them?"

"Well, not exactly! But one Friday night, when Reza was coming home from the tube station, he saw that the group was harassing a half-drunk girl in a park. There were a few other passersby also in the streets, but they didn't want to get intervene."

"But Reza jumped to her aid, did he?" I ask.

"Yes, he did. He was that kind of a person. Ben and his gang first asked him to sod off and mind his own business."

"Which he didn't, I suppose?"

"No, that was not him. Instead, he shouted, threatened to call the police and in the meanwhile a few more passersby gathered. So, Ben and his gang had to backtrack. But before leaving he threatened Reza to be prepared for the 'consequences', which was heard by at least five witnesses present there." Neil finishes telling the story.

"Sounds like an empty threat to me." I commented.

"Yeah, to me too. Definitely not enough to get hold of thallium and go to his lab to mix it in his teapot." Neil agrees with me.

"But Daniel thinks they actually took revenge on Reza?"

"Yep. Unfortunately, that's what he thinks," Neil nods.

"That's bonkers, Neil! How could they possibly have done it? They came to Reza's lab, mixed the thallium in his pot, made him drink it and then left? Without anyone noticing it? Without getting snapped by the CCTV cameras? It just doesn't add up, Neil."

"Well, a lot doesn't add up here, Sri. The broken piece of that teapot, which you and I retrieved from the trash after so much hassle; I am pretty sure we can get a lot of forensic evidence from it if we get it tested thoroughly. But they are not even sending it to the forensic lab."

Well, this is a new and disturbing piece of information. After we took so much pain to retrieve the piece from the garbage, the least I expected is a forensic test of that piece. Why was even that denied? Even if the result is negative, that would vindicate Daniel's theory, wouldn't it?

"I see. So, all this, running up and down the country in disguise, is this your personal side project? Nothing official about it?" I finally ask Neil.

"To some extent, yes. Honestly, I lost all faith when they did not send that broken piece to the forensic lab. I can no longer give them the benefit of doubt." Neil finally admits it, which he was very hesitant to do until now.

"Obviously. Even if they think it is thallium, still it has to be tested to be sure."

"I think they are sure it is not thallium, and they don't want others to find out what it really is. That's why they are trying to divert the direction of this investigation."

"What do you mean, Neil? Whom are you suspecting?"

"Daniel was asking me all sorts of questions about you. Who you are, what do you do, why are you involved in this case, how did you find the teapot, what did you do after that, who else did you speak to etc. etc. He even ordered a background check on you."

"Background check! I have heard the term, but what is it, exactly?"

"They will look into everything. Your visa status, your grades in the college, your bank details, your social media accounts, everything. They would find out everything about you; where you do your shopping, where do you get your takeaways from, who you hang out with, who you are sleep with…"

"…Shut up Neil!"

"Well, that really is the case. I told you because you asked. It is the truth".

It is a scary truth to be honest. It is the big brother state on steroids.

"But what about you, Neil? How long can you be on the run? Are you not expected to show up in the office?"

"Our duty is not regular nine to five, Sri. We often go incognito or undercover. That's the nature of our job. In fact, Daniel gave me another case to handle a couple of days ago—possibly to divert my attention from this case. I told him that I will be in Wiltshire, incognito and out of communication, to investigate that case."

"How long can you keep this going?"

"Not for long, I am afraid. May be a couple of more days, max." Neil sounds tired as he rubs his eyes.

The situation looks a lot grimmer than I thought it to be. Previously, even though it was scary, at least I thought MI6 is behind us. But now it seems that we are on our own. Neil has taken a huge risk and is banking on us cracking the case soon. I, on the other hand am on the bullseye for the ruthless foreign spies.

"Don't you have any other friend in your department?" I ask after a pause.

"Yes, I have. Mirella. She is in message deciphering unit."

I remember the name Mirella, Suparna talked about her. Neil's friend and colleague.

"I see. Is she also like Suparna? Works with cyber security?" I ask.

"Not exactly. Sups has a background in Computer Science, she is a white hat hacker. Mirella on the other hand is a linguist. They work with decoding and deciphering of the tapped messages. They have recently intercepted a few interesting, coded messages."

"From Iran?" I hazard a guess.

"No, from Russia, actually."

"Blimey! How does Russia come into the picture?"

"Russia and Iran are aligned. Just as we and the USA are aligned," Neil smiles.

"And Syria's Asad regime also have their support, right?"

"Yes, they do. If not always openly, then definitely under the radar."

Both of us sit in silence for a while. I have a lot of info to process in my head. Then I ask again, "This colleague of yours, Mirella, is she also young, like you?"

Neil was probably not expecting this question, so he sounds a little surprised when he answers. "Y-yes, she is roughly my age. Why do you ask?"

"The things which look suspicious to juniors like you and Mirella, how come your boss, with the years of experience under his belt, doesn't find them disturbing?"

"He… perhaps he doesn't want a lot of trouble now, he wants peace and is looking for a simple solution. He is on the verge of his retirement, you see!"

"No, I don't see, Neil. He is in MI6, in a fairly high up position. He should know more than anyone that simple solutions to a crime don't always exist. Retirement or no retirement, he should dig things when they are this suspicious. You, me, Mirella we can all see it, why not him?"

"Sri, what you are insinuating is very grave," Neil's voice is grim.

"Tell me Neil, don't you think it, too?" I charge him point blank.

This time Neil takes a while to answer. Then he speaks again, "Yes, it came to my mind, too. But it doesn't matter what we think. Our suspicion is not enough. We need evidence. Hard evidence."

"That silver car which spooked you so much that we left Royston in such a hurry, leaving all our belongings and the rented car there, it was from your department, right?" I speculate.

"Right. That one is our car and Craig uses it these days. Craig Tulley, our number one sniper."

"I see! Does he snipe his own colleagues?"

"He would if he gets the order. That's all he cares about, the order. Nothing else."

This is getting more and more complicated and dangerous, as I can see. Now we are being chased by a professional sniper.

"How did they know that you were in Royston?"

"Not sure! Maybe from the credit card, I used to pay the hotel in the morning…"

"Or could be from your phone," I suggest.

"I am not using any SIM, Sri. I am just using secure messaging apps like Signal and Telegram while logged into Wi-Fi. Matt also messaged me in Signal. I have also installed Nord VPN for secure browsing."

"Does Matt have a Signal account? Didn't know that!"

"Everybody uses it these days. You should install it too. Way more secure."

Of course, it is secure, and Matt seems to be quite keen of secrecy and security. A few things don't add up there, either. But let us concentrate on the present problem first.

"I will install it as soon as I am allowed to use my phone again." I promise and then continue, "But tell me one thing, that black car that came to your flat in London, was it also from your department?"

"No, Sri. At least as far as I know, it is not. But my suspicion is this was from FSB."

"What is the FSB?" I have never heard of it.

"The Russian spy agency. What used to be known as the KGB before." Neil smiles.

"Has the KGB changed its name? Never knew it." I admitted.

"Yes, the KGB ceased to exist in 1991. The new reincarnation is FSB. The name changed, but nothing else changed much. It still is the same organization with same modus operandi."

"But how did you know that the black car was from FSB? Do they register the number plates under FSB?"

"No, that would be very stupid, and they are anything but stupid." Neil smiles again and then continues, "I didn't recognize the number plate, but I did recognize the man, who was walking towards us from the opposite direction, near the park. Remember?"

How can I ever forget! "That man, because of whom you forced me to kiss you?"

"Forced you? Did I have choice, Sri? I was just trying to save both of our lives. Perhaps I shouldn't have. I should have let Andrei catch you. He would have killed you in ten seconds for sure, but so what? You would die all chaste and pure."

Neil sounds mighty angry!

"Andrei? Do you know him?" I continued with my questions.

"He is not my friend, obviously! But yes, I know him. Andrei Tonkovich is an FSB agent, fairly well known to us. He often visits London for 'work'."

"Strange! Why don't you arrest him, then?"

## Alpha Beta Gamma

"You need a reason, a proof, to arrest somebody, Sri. He comes on a valid visa, doesn't do anything illegal, so how can we arrest him? There are many who we suspect or even know to be foreign agents, but we cannot arrest them unless they do something illegal on our soil. Just gathering information is not an arrestable offence, I am afraid. So, all we can do is watch them."

"I see. So that day, if you didn't kiss me, then Andrei would have killed me. Then you would have enough proof to arrest him."

"Right! I should have used you as the bait. Made a serious mistake saving you, it seems." Neil is being sarcastic.

Before I can ask my next question, Neil's phone starts ringing. A voice call comes on Signal.

"Yes, Sups, tell me."

Neil puts the phone on speaker and gestures to me to sit beside him.

"Neil, I did progress a little with that message hacking," Suparna sounds excited.

"Really? What did you get?" Neil asks.

"It is serious, Neil. Most likely you have a mole in your department, who is working as a Russian double agent."

"Who? What is his name?"

"I don't know yet. It was not very clear from the hacked messages; they were very careful in communicating, never used the full names of the people. And anyway, we should not discuss all these over the phone. Wasn't your phone bugged a couple of days ago?"

"Hmm. So how do you want to tell me?"

"I can go to your apartment, and we can talk face to face."

"But I am not in London now."

"Oh! Where are you? Or is it confidential?"

"Actually, it's fieldwork, so …"

"Confidential. I get it. So, let's talk when you are back then. By the way, how was the *kheer* that day? Did you share it with Sri?"

Neil and I look at each other. Then Neil replies, "It was very good. I shared it with Sri, too."

"That's great. Neil, one thing, about Sri…"

"Yes Sups, what is it?" Neil asks, keeping his eyes on me.

"Look, I never give you any advice, but I want to tell you something today…" Suparna sounds hesitant.

"Yes, Sups… go on… I am listening."

"Sri is a very good girl. So please handle her with care. I know you have those commitment issues… does she know about them?"

"Yes, I think she knows. But why are you asking, Sups?" Neil sounds a little annoyed.

"Nothing! She came across a bit old school to me, I mean when it comes to relationships and all. So, I'm just asking you to be careful not to hurt her. I know that you won't do it intentionally, but just be mindful not to cause any unintentional harm. That's all I had to say."

"What do you think, Sri?" Neil asks me after putting the phone down.

"She is either innocent or is a very shrewd actress." I give my honest reply.

"Which one do you think is it?" Neil asks again.

"Innocent."

"Obviously. Because she gave you the certificate of good girl."

"I am a good girl, and everyone knows that! I don't need any certificate to prove it. But if she is not innocent then why would she tell you about the double agent?"

"It is now clear to our enemies that I am suspecting a double agent. So, this could be a ploy to gain my confidence. Give a bit of already known information and gain trust—a very old technique," Neil says in a dark voice.

"Hmm… complicated. So, your phone is clean now, right?"

"I hope so! I reinstalled everything the other day. Didn't I tell you?"

"Yes, you told me. You re-installed it that day when you were with Anthea—"

"Jesus, will you keep harping about Anthea for the rest of my life?"

"Rest of your life? Why? Why would I be there to bother you for the rest of your life?" "That's just a figure of speech. Don't read too much into it," Neil clarifies himself hastily. But for the first-time, street-smart Neil Basu looks a bit off guard.

## *Alpha Beta Gamma*

Next morning, we get up and have breakfast. I can see Neil is getting impatient, time is running out for him, for us both, actually. Perhaps he is waiting for some more information and proof from Mirella or Suparna. I am not sure if he has any other sources to help him. At around nine o'clock, Neil goes out to make an urgent call. So, I decide to have a little walk in the village by myself. I take Neil's private phone with me. It is my only way to communicate with the world these days. Even this I need to keep switched off, barring any emergencies.

    This is a pretty little English village, very picturesque. Creeper roses or ivy on the walls of old, quaint, thatched roofed cottages, quiet streets and alleys, a church spire s visible at a distance. Green paddocks and meadows can be seen at the end of the village. The river Cam must be nearby. I start walking towards it. This is a sleepy little village with empty streets, so not much risk of being seen by our enemies, I suppose.

# Malabika Ray

The meadows in November are a bit dull, already having lost quite a bit of their green summer hues. Still, the air is fresh and crisp, carrying the subtle scents of the late blooming wild roses and the earthy aroma of the fields. The greenish black water of Cam reflects the dull November sky, with a pair of swans gliding gracefully across the surface.

I get a little alarmed, because no matter how majestic and graceful they look I know for a fact that those Swans are very aggressive, because I was chased by them on my last visit to Cambridge.

I came to Cambridge a few months back, to meet my friend Shamik, who is doing his Masters at Darwin College. He hired a punt boat, and we punted up to this village of Grantchester. I quite liked the narrow, small river Cam with the weeping willows drooping on both sides. The only drawbacks there were those aggressive swans who chase random people without any provocation whatsoever.

As I am walking by the river, many thoughts come to my mind. How long could we be on the run like this? My college, studies, my whole life is on hold now. I could not contact my parents, no one can contact me either as I have taken the SIM out of my phone. Matt, Sadia, my other friends, or Aunt Shukla—everyone will soon start worrying about me, and for very good reasons. What if mum gets super worried and asks Aunt Shukla to check on me? If she drops by or calls Matt and finds out that I am absconding for days, she will go to the police for sure. And here I am, absconded with a policeman. The irony!

I come back to the hotel in half an hour. Just before entering, though, I remember that I did not reply to Matt and Sadia's birthday wish. I cannot call them of course, but it might be a good idea to record a video message and send it to them. This could actually be a good idea because they will be less worried about me. So, I just record a small thank you message and send it from Neil's personal phone, using the hotel's Wi-Fi. I tell them that I dopped my phone and it is now broken and hence they can't reach me there.

Coming back to the room, I find Neil in a sombre mood.
"What's the matter Neil?" I ask.
"I talked to Mirella. She contacted the Guardian journalist."

"Who, Mary Mason? Did she agree to speak to you guys? Usually, those investigative journalists are fiercely protective of their sources, aren't they?" I ask.

"True. The free press is very important in this country. But in this particular case, Mary did help somewhat. Maybe because the source is already dead, and we are trying to investigate his murder. They also know that other people might also be in danger if the murderer remains at loose. Like Helena."

"I see! So, Reza and Mary Mason were in close contact just days before his death, right? I think that's explains Reza being busy and spending a lot of time in front of his computer and talking about a deadline." I mention.

"Who told you about his deadline and submissions, Sri?"

"Irene, Reza's wife. Initially I thought he was probably working on some scientific paper. Irene thought that, too." I clarify.

"Was he not?" Neil asks.

"No. Not at that point in time. I checked with other professors and the PhD and post-doctoral students who used to collaborate with Reza. None of them mentioned any in-progress paper just prior to his death." I say.

"Hmm. Then Reza probably was busy gathering evidence for Mary Mason and submitting it to some secure server. Possibly Secure Drop." Neil's deduction seems to be quite convincing.

"Anyway, what did Mary Mason tell Mirella?" I ask.

"Reza obviously got killed before he could give her any evidence. But the interesting thing is, Reza apparently told Mary the secret information could be embarrassing not just for Iran, but for Russia, too."

"How so?"

"Because this would shed the light on Russia's connection with Asad and how he used illegal Sarin gas on his own civilians."

"You mean the gas killing? The one at Ghouta in Syria, in 2013?"

"Yes, that's the one."

"My God! That was terrible. How many kids got killed? Those photos and videos of children suffering… terrible."

"I know. This would be a major embarrassment for Russia because they always denied any connection with that ghastly incident. It could possibly be a war crime and UN would act. A lot of countries in the West always suspected the connection, but they never had enough proof."

"The UN can do nothing because Russia has the veto power. But that is beside the point. So, what you are implying is, not just Iran, but Russia also has stakes to stop Reza from sharing the information with the journalists," I infer.

"Exactly, Ms. Marple. And Russia is a much bigger power with a much more dangerous and reckless spy network. They have already sent spies to this country to kill people on our soil."

"Humm. Litvinenko's radiation poisoning in the sushi bar and then the Salisbury poisoning of Skripal father and daughter." I mention the two most notorious incident of spying in recent times.

"Yes. There is no reason to think that they cannot do it for a third time. I can bet FSB and Iranian intelligence are working together on this."

Neil sounds confident and I have to agree with him too. But the theory or the suspicion alone is not enough. We need proof.

"Neil, the message that Mirella tapped, did it by any chance mention any murder weapon?" I know it's a long shot, still I try my luck.

"No. They only mentioned some 'perfect poison'. The message was at least three weeks old. According to that tapped message, two Russian agents, Andrei and Ivan, were supposed to come to London with the 'perfect poison' and contact their local friends here, an 'S and M'"

"S and M? Who are they?" I ask.

"No idea, Sri." Neil throws his hands apart.

"Hmm, interesting. This is a multifaceted problem, it seems."

"Obviously. Three unknowns… Alpha, Beta, Gamma… The murderer weapon, the mole in MI6 and S and M…" Neil is thinking aloud.

True. Alpha, Beta, Gamma. Three unknowns. If Alpha is the murder weapon—

—My God! Oh, my god!

Yes, exactly… that is why… of course! It is all falling in place.

Damn, I should have guessed before, how could I be so stupid?

"Neil, I think I know the murder weapon." I am very excited.

"What?" Neil is startled.

"Yes. It is polonium-210. A radioactive isotope of polonium," I say in a firm tone, as I am dead sure about it.

"Sri, we talked about it before. How could it be? The substance is radioactive, right? How come then nothing was detected in the Geiger Counter?" Neil sounds a little impatient.

"That's exactly what I am saying Neil. Polonium-210 is a very special kind of radioactive substance. It can't be detected by the Geiger."

"Why?" Neil is still confused.

"Come on Neil, you also studied Physics at Uni. Tell me, how does the Geiger Counter work? What does it measure?"

"It measures the ionization rate of the air." Neil answers correctly.

"Ionization by what, Neil?"

"By Gamma radiation, emitted by all radioactive substance."

"No, Neil, no. Not all radioactive substances emit Gamma rays. That's where we went wrong. Most of them do, but not all. Some emit Alpha particles. Like polonium-210."

Neil is silent for a moment. He is processing the info. His eyes soon begin to twinkle.

"Right Sri, you are absolutely right. That must be it. Geiger does not detect Alpha emission. A slightly higher reading that you found in the teapot was due to the fact that polonium emits very little, about ten percent, gamma rays. That's what was detected by the Geiger."

"Correct, Neil. It had nothing to do with the low half-life. But that broken piece of teapot can now serve as the strongest evidence."

"Absolutely. If our forensic does a scintillation test on that broken piece of that teapot, then the polonium poisoning of Reza can be proved beyond any doubt." Now Neil is excited, too.

"Yes, Neil, everything is falling in place. Polonium-210, is nicknamed the perfect poison. Two billion times deadlier than the cyanide. A few drops in the teapot, and anyone drinking that poison potion will die within a few hours. Alpha emitters have lot of advantages…"

"Absolutely, Sri. Alpha particles have very low penetration power. So, unlike gamma rays, they do not travel far through the air. Everything, like skin or clothes will act as barrier. That's why the person who carries the alpha emitter has almost no risk of getting contaminated. Again, unlike gamma rays, which can travel miles to affect people."

Neil is now very excited and is pacing the room up and down.

## Alpha Beta Gamma

"You are right, Neil. Carrying polonium is easy and Risk free. Unlike gamma emitting radioactive substance like radium, it will not have to be carried in a lead container. One can just dissolve it in water and carry a small glass vial of that deadly liquid easily in his pocket. He will breeze through any airport security in the world," I remind him.

"Right. Polonim-210 does not pose any threat to simple contact with the skin or clothes. But if it enters the bloodstream, then it becomes deadly. Just a couple of drops from that vial will be enough. Once swallowed, every alpha particle will hit the body cells with more than five mega electron volts of energy. It will be like atomic blasts in individual cells. Which will lead to multi-organ failure within a few hours. It will fatally affect the central nervous system, the GI tract. These symptoms are to some extent similar to thallium poisoning." Neil correctly points out.

"Exactly. The murderer entered Reza's lab that day with the polonium vial in his pocket and must have poured a few drops from the vial into the teapot when no one was looking. Fairly simple." I conjecture.

"Right. Nothing will appear on CCTV or in DNA analysis. Because the murderer must have been someone who goes to that lab every day. A faculty or a student or an admin or a cleaner. And most likely he mixed the poison with the tea when Reza was still alive, possibly was still working. So, it is futile to look for somebody who went in there just before Reza died."

Neil is also trying the put all the pieces together in this puzzle.

"That means Reza was indeed alone when he died. That explains no forensic evidence of any struggle with the murderer," I comment.

"So, it seems. Now the only thing that remains. What is 138?" Neil asks.

For a moment I can't understand what he means, but then I remember quickly. He was referring to the paper in Reza's hand.

Reza wrote 210-138 on a piece of paper before he died, and 210 is the mass number of the polonium isotope which emits alpha particles. What the hell is 138 then?

"Could it be the half-life of polonium? Google it!" I hypothesize.

"Yes, it is! Brilliant, Sri!" Neil looks it up quickly and confirms. Polonium-210 has a half-life of 138 days.

"So, Reza did understand that he was poisoned. Not only that, but he also suspected it probably was polonium-210. Most likely from the symptoms. He knew that he was dying, so he wanted to leave a clue. He must have passed out before writing anything more. But he did leave an important clue, the scientific identifier of the murder weapon. He was a true scientist till his last breath." I feel sad as I say this.

"Ok, so now we know what the murder weapon is. One problem, alpha, is solved, out of the three. We still have two more to go. Beta and Gamma. The mole in our department and the S&M duo."

Neil was already thinking of the next steps.

"Who is the murderer then? One of these S and M?" I ask.

"Could be. One of them could be the murderer and the other could be the double agent who is helping him."

"So, what do you do now, Neil? Call your boss?"

Even though I ask it, I did not think it was going to be a very useful question. But thankfully Neil says, "No Sri, Daniel will not help me, he is fixated with his simple murder theory. But now I have a lot of information and evidence. So, I will go to our Cambridge office and will talk to our department officials face to face. Daniel is not the only person who decides everything in MI6. There have got to be other sane voices who could order a proper investigation and forensic tests. Especially when there are mounting evidence and compelling theories to back them. Our days on the run will soon be over, Sri."

Neil sounds determined.

\*\*\*

Neil left about forty-five minutes back. He left his private phone for me, so that I can contact him in case of an emergency. He puts a brand new SIM in his personal mobile and asks me to keep it with me, in case he needs to call or text me. I was thinking of S and M. Local accomplice of FSB. Who could they be?

Matt? Mirella?

Suparna? Sadia? Aunt Shukla?

Even in these tense circumstances, the thought of Aunt Shukla being an FSB agent really makes me laugh hard. I picture her on the other end of the big table with the president, giving instructions to ruthless spies... in which language by the way?

My comedy daydream gets interrupted as Neil's phone beeps. A text message comes through.

"Sri, this is Neil. Could you please come by the river Cam? Mirella has got some new information. We might be able to nail the Mole. She wants to talk to you," the message read. It comes from Neil's work phone. Could I trust this? His phone was bugged before, then he cleaned it up, reinstalled everything there. Could they bug it again? So soon?

On the other hand, it could be true. Maybe he and Mirella have found some clue regarding S and M and they need my help. Is this a risk worth taking? Perhaps!

"Hi Neil, where exactly by the river Cam?"

"If you come out of the hotel and cross the road then you will see a big, green field. Just walk across the field for about ten minutes, you will see the river. The place is locally known as the Little Meadow. There, you will find a boat moored under a pair of twin weeping willow trees. We will be there on that boat."

"Why are you in there? Why don't you come here, in our hotel?" I ask.

"This is our boat, Sri, our department's. Mirella is also here. It is much safer in there. Please come over."

"OK, I am coming."

Alright, if this message is indeed from the bad guys, then they already know where I am. So, it is not going to help much if I stay put. If they are after me, then they can get me in here, this B&B is hardly a fortress. It is better to go there and take the chance. There is a risk, for sure, but then sleuthing is a risky business, even more so for the sloppy sleuths.

I go downstairs and confirm the direction for the Little Meadows from reception. It's a little bit to the left of where I went for walk in the morning. I start waking, following that direction. The text message says it is about ten minutes' walk. The meadow is really nice and scenic. There is a big animal paddock nearby. Lots of big cows are grazing there. I keep walking, keeping an eye on those scary cows and making sure not to step on any cow dung or other animal shit.

I reach the river in eleven minutes. Calling this a river seems to be an exaggeration. In India, we wouldn't even call it a rivulet. But it's not all about the size. The town of Cambridge gets its name from this tiny waterbody and all those world-famous colleges—Kings', Trinity, St. Johns'—are on the bank of this river, the students of which do punting in this river in the summer.

Just two hundred meters away, on the left-hand side, I find the twin weeping willows. Under them, a narrow but covered boat is moored. The boat has a cute flag in it, red, yellow, and blue with a picture of hawk flying on the roof. I could not see any soul nearby, except for those scary cows at a distance and two angry looking Swans in the water.

I go towards the boat. The door is not locked, it opens as I pushed it. I go inside. There are a few stairs going down to a big, open space. But the hall is empty.

"Neil!" I shout.

"Welcome, Sri! We were waiting for you."
The voice comes from behind. I turn around.

## *The Climax*

"Professor Kowalski! So, you are the Russian spy!" I exclaim.

"Yes, for a long time now. This kind of job at a Uni is very safe, you see. No one suspected a thing in all these years." The professor gives a complacent smile.

Professor Alexander Kowalski. Alexander is nicknamed as Sasha in Russia. So, he is the S.

I keep thinking of Neil. That day while coming back from his dad's house in Islington he mentioned, 'we sometimes give alternate identities to our spies.' This is probably a common practice in all spy agencies across the world.

"Obviously, I had the qualifications. I have a PhD from the Moscow University. The FSB did help with other testimonials and recommendations. We are lot more efficient than your Western intelligent agencies." Kowalski brags.

"So, the message that I received from Neil's phone—"

"Nah, he didn't send it. It was us. We hacked his phone, again." He laughs.

"Didn't he reinstall everything on his phone just a few days back?"

"He did. But when he called again this morning and gave his theory on the polonium poisoning and asked for a scintillation test of the broken piece of that teapot, then we had to act quickly. So, we hacked it again!"

"But Neil only told his colleagues about it!"

"What do you think Sri, don't we have our people in MI6?" Kowalski smiles.

"Senior Detective Daniel Morgan! Neil's boss. S and M— Sasha and Morgan." I exclaim.

The professor gives another of his complacent smiles and then says, "How did you know about S and M? Did you tap Andrei and Ivan's messages?"

"Everyone in MI6 is not compromised, thankfully! Some still do their job with honesty and integrity." I reply.

"Yes, they do," Kowalski said in a cool, matter-of-fact voice.

"But both you and Neil made the same mistake, you poked the hornet's nest. This is way bigger than either of you. Spy agencies of three different countries are involved here. How could you even think that a junior detective and a college student can take them on?"

I remain silent. The professor keeps talking, "To be honest, I have nothing against you personally, Sri. You are a good student, came from a foreign country. You should have stuck to your studies and not poke your nose in this international spy business. You could have had a shining career. But you threw everything away to be a sleuth. What a pity!" The professor shakes his head and then speaks again, "Your problem is your curiosity, my dear. You are way too curious. That day, when I saw the Geiger near the teapot, I sensed that you suspected something. I knew that Geiger would not catch anything—polonium 210 is mainly an alpha emitter, it hardly emits any gamma rays. So, there was no immediate danger of our plan getting exposed, still I understood from that very moment that you need to be kept under watch."

"That's why you broke the teapot, didn't you? To destroy the evidence" I ask.
"Yeah, if I just removed the pot, people would have been suspicious; I mean who steals an old teapot? That's why I broke it, so that it looked like an accident; ceramic teapots break all the time. Then I collected the broken pieces in a plastic bag and instead of throwing them in trash, I put it in the boot of my car. I thought, that's that."
"But you made a small mistake, professor, one piece was hidden under the counter which Natalia found while cleaning and threw in the trash," I remind him.

"Small mistake, yes. But even that would have been fine if you did not poke your nose in there, too. Never thought you would scavenge the garbage to fish a broken piece out. You brought all this danger on yourself, Sri. You have only yourself to blame."

Interesting logic and victim blaming at its finest, I think. "So, you started planning to kill me from that day, is it, Professor Kowalski?"

"Naturally. I have got that vial of poloium-210. First, I thought I will put it your coffee once you are back in the lab. But after that garbage scavenging incident, you never came back to the college."

A chill goes down my spine. I would have gone back to Kowalski's lab if Neil hadn't forbidden me to do so and I would have drunk a poisonous cup of coffee soon after that. I owe my life to him, it seems!

"Did you tap my phone after that? With the help of your friend, Mr. Morgan?"

"Obviously. My friend Morgan is much higher up and hence much more influential than your friend Neil, Sri. He ordered a background check on you. If he could find anything—any small thing, like an unpaid bill or visa irregularities or an unpaid parking ticket, he would have nabbed you. But unfortunately for us, your records were clean. Then we had no choice but to tap your phone. Morgan ordered legal interception, citing a security threat," Kowalski smiles.

"But I kept my phone switched off. I even took the SIM out."

"Yes, you did. That was clever. Who advised you? Neil? We got delayed by a day or so in finding you. Our spies watched your flat in Canning Town. They even went to your aunt's house in Wimbledon but could not find you there. We did not really think Neil would bring you to his own apartment. It's a huge risk, really, and he should have known. Usually, people working in national spy agencies don't do that. But Neil is young, perhaps has some kind of feelings for you and that is why took this big risk. It was our mistake to overlook this possibility."

"How did you finally find my location?"

"When you switched on your WhatsApp. Morgan had already given the order and we got the WhatsApp metadata. Then our team of hacking experts managed to nail your location within an hour or so. We did not waste any time, our people were there in front of Neil's house soon after that, but you were already gone. Again, Neil helped you, I suppose. Without him, you would not stand a chance against Andrei," he said bluntly.

I remain silent. Kowalski looks at and me and smiles, "I am feeling bad, you see! Like a movie villain, I am getting in the way of budding love between two young souls…" his tone is clearly sarcastic.

THAT's why he thinks himself a villain? Not because of spying or killing his two colleagues or conspiring to kill his own student! Some people have really crooked minds.

"What about Helena, Professor? Why did you kill her?" I ask. This is still a mystery to me. Why did they have to kill harmless, dull Helena like this?

"I didn't kill Helena, Sri! At least not intentionally." Kowalski has a mysterious smile on his lips.

"Then?"

"Then what? Do I need to tell you everything? You are the sleuth, figure it out yourself! Anyway, none of this will be of any use to you or the Police. You can ask Helena about it yourself, when you join her in the afterlife soon."

His smile widens. 'Not intentionally', probably that means she was indeed collateral damage. But how? I kept thinking. Her fingers, the bald patch on her head, the common wall separating the pantry counter in Reza's lab and the diffraction setup in Helena's lab. Perhaps I know how she was killed; I do not have to ask her in afterlife. In fact, I have no intention of joining her there anytime soon. I have to figure a way out to escape this killer professor. I have to keep a cool head.

"Did your man, Andrei, poison a dessert in Neil's flat when we were out?" I ask Kowalski.

"No, Andrei did not enter Neil's flat, my dear. It was Morgan's people. When the lobby manager told our guys that you and Neil went out for the birthday celebration, then first we checked with Morgan. He looked through the official records and confirmed it was indeed Neil's birthday. So, we just took a chance, in case you came back that night… we just wanted to foolproof everything, you see. But unfortunately, that did not work. You and Neil never returned to his flat night but fled London. When we were busy poisoning that blasted dessert, you were already in Royston." He sounds a little annoyed at the missed chance of killing us.

"How did you know about Royston, professor?"

"Credit card! MI6 can do a lot of things if they want to. That's the reason we spent millions of dollars to buy Morgan. You have no idea, my child, how much money he has in the tax heaven of Panama. Sometimes it makes me jealous, too. Andrei, Ivan and I, we do all the heavy liftings, and he reaps the benefit purely because of his position. It is so unfair." Kowalski lets out a dry laugh.

Criminal psychology is indeed a strange thing. I read it somewhere—possibly in Tolstoy's *Resurrection*—that it is our misconception to think that most criminals are always ridden with guilt. That is not true at all. Everyone finds a justification for what they do. Otherwise, they would not be able to continue doing it. That is their survival mechanism. It is probably not that different from the world leaders who give orders to bomb 'enemy' cities wiping out the entire civilian population there.

Anyways, this is not the time to ponder on the theory of criminal psychology. I need to figure out what this killer is planning to do with me. True, my position looks rather bleak at the moment, but I cannot really give up, can I? I also have to find my own survival mechanism.

"So, what are your plans with me, Professor Kowalski?" I ask.

"I am sorry, Sri, but I think you are destined for this. I never thought you would be the next recipient of it, but as I said earlier, you brought it upon yourself."

He takes a small glass vial out of his pocket. I immediately understand that the transparent liquid inside is polonium-210 dissolved in water. The perfect poison. A billion times deadlier than the cyanide.

"Now I will inject this into you."

He takes out a syringe from his pocket this time and then continues, "In a few hours, we will put your dead body in your room in the Nag's Head. Then Morgan will make sure to frame Neil for your abduction and murder."

Kowalski gives a very satisfying smile. It is a good plan indeed. Murdering one enemy and framing the other one for the same murder. Perhaps they will also put the polonium vial in our room in the Nag's Head. Then they can frame Neil as the Russian mole in MI6. That he used me—a love stricken, naïve girl—to kill Reza, because I had access to him and his lab. Then Neil killed me to eliminate the witness. All the evidence—the broken teapot piece, Mirella's tapped messages—everything would very conveniently be used against us. It is a perfect screenplay.

"I don't think you are going to put up a lot of fight, Sri, still, I must warn you. Don't try to do anything clever, it is not going to help. I don't want to put you through unnecessary suffering, so I have adjusted the dose in such a way that the whole thing will be quick. Sergei…"

Kowalski calls someone. A huge giant of a man comes from the next room. He is at least six and half feet tall, very muscular, like a bodybuilder, and he also has a gun in his hand.

I almost feel like laughing. Such an elaborate arrangement to kill me? For the Sloppy Sleuth? What can I possibly do? I don't know how to use a gun, I know no martial arts. I am five feet three, weigh fifty-six kilos, I wear minus powered glasses. Sergei on the other hand is at least twice my size, has the build of a wrestler, his biceps visible even from under his shirt.

Two killers, a gun, and a vial of deadly poison… the odds are hugely stacked against me. I stand no chance against them physically. My only chance is my brain. Let me try… I have nothing to lose anyway!

"Professor Kowalski, if you kill me, you will never get the documents that the Iranian ex-spy Nasser Ali gave to Reza for sharing with Guardian's investigative journalist, Mary Mason. These are the documents for which you literally killed. Don't you want them back?"

I take my chances. Kowalski stops for a moment and looks at me, frowning. Then he asks, "What are you trying to say, Sri?"

"I am trying to bargain. I can give you those documents if you spare my life."

I have started playing the dangerous game of poker with my life at stake.

"Where are those documents? In your hotel room? In the Nag's Head?"

The professor took my first bluff, it seems. It has become quite clear to me that Kowalski is a bit old school. Why would either Nasser Ali or Reza or the investigative journalist Marry Mason keep such sensitive information in physical copy? It is way too dangerous.

"No, professor! These days no one carries such sensitive data in hard copy. They are there in soft copy." I continue with my ingenious bluff.

"Where, in Reza's laptop?"

Sasha Kowalski's computer knowledge is primitive. That's a known thing in our department. He never let us do our assignments online, never uses any slides or software presentations while teaching us. He even uses a printed log table, instead of using a scientific calculator. And that incident of 'losing his mouse' which Mike told us about the other day. It was hilarious, really. He could not find the cursor in his computer and asked Mike for help. Now this is my chance to see if I can use this weakness of his to my advantage.

"No, professor. These days no one keeps important data on their hard disks. They can get corrupted or the whole laptop can be stolen or destroyed by accident. People normally keep them in some secure online platform."

At least this is a generic truth which professor finds convincing enough and asks, "Would you be able to access it?"

"I think I can. If I can get a computer and an internet connection." I am betting heavily on my ingenuity and Kowalski's naivety with modern technology.

"Alright then. I will give you my computer and a data connection. If you can give me those documents, I will spare your life," Kowalski agrees.

"Will you really let me go after I give you the documents?"

"Yeah, why not? Without those documents no one will believe you or Neil. Even if they believe, they will not be able to prove anything. So, there would be no reason for me to kill you then. Killings are cumbersome, you see. I don't want to take that trouble unless it is absolutely necessary." He lets out a dry laugh.

I know Sasha Kowalski is lying. He would kill me, even if I gave him the documents, because I know too much. I know that he actually is an FSB spy, I know that he killed Reza and I also know that Daniel Morgan, Neil's boss is an FSB double agent working in MI6. No one will let me go free with this kind of bombshell information.

He must be thinking that he will kill me as soon as I hand the documents over to him. He has the weapon, he has Sergei. And me? What am I thinking? Not sure, really. I am just improvising.

I have no idea where Reza's documents are actually kept. What I need right now is a computer, an internet connection, and some time, as much time as I can get.

I presume the documents from Nasser Ali are uploaded in Secure Drop. It is an open-source, secure, whistleblower submission system news organizations can install to safely and anonymously receive documents and tips from their sources. This is the most common one, which is used by whistleblowers all over the world to anonymously tip investigative journalists. The Guardian also uses Secure Drop, Even Edward Snowden used it to release his dossier. Reza could very well have his own Secure Drop account, but I do not have the skills to hack that, for sure. But I have to fake it. I have to make professor believe that I am actually hacking it.

"Professor Kowalski, normally people keep these kinds of secret documents in Secure Drop. That is a highly secure platform. I will try to hack Reza's account there. But it will take some time." I keep my poker face.

"How long?" The professor is frowning.

"Not sure… forty-forty-five minutes, I guess."

"Alright. But not more than that. If you cannot hack it and give me the documents by then, I will have no other choice than to…" The professor does not finish his sentence, but just shows the glass vial to me again.

I swallow the chilling threat in silence and start working on Kowalski's laptop. First, I create a Tor browser and a Secure Drop account. Then I open a command prompt in the laptop and start a few random, benign commands like ping and route trace. These are for camouflage. A computer naïf like Kowalski would think I am running some sophisticated hacking attempts.

My main objective is to open Signal and to send an SOS to Neil. They have hacked Neil's work phone. If I use normal SMS or WhatsApp, they will be able to read them. But they cannot read encrypted Signal messages. I am sure Neil has a screen lock setting on in his Signal App. That will prevent the hackers from device reading.

Kowalski is looking at my screen. As soon as I started downloading Signal, he grew suspicious and asked,

"What is it?"

"It is a secure messaging application, connected to the Secure Drop." I keep bluffing.

"Why do you need it?" He is still suspicious.

"I am trying to find the communication between Reza and the Guardian journalist." I am improvising left, right and centre. The professor looks at ease again. He must have been convinced by this lie.

I start a few SQL injections from my newly created accounts. Standing behind me, Prof. Kowalski is looking at my screen and observing my every action. He seems impressed. Good for me.

"What are you doing, Sri?" Kowalski's tone is full of awe and curiosity.

"Creating some sequel injections to hack Reza's account," I reply.

"Yes, yes! I have heard of these. You can hack everything with SQL injection." He sounds excited.

No, you can't hack everything with SQL injection. That's a misconception. Only very poorly designed systems with weak security mechanisms can be hacked this way. Definitely not the modern, state of the art, high secure platforms like Secure Drop. But it is good that our old school, killer professor does not know about it. I have to keep playing this game keeping my poker face straight.

Now I have a to figure out a way to message Neil that will not make this killer professor suspicious. He is standing right behind me and reading every single word I am typing. So, I cannot write the message in plain English. Kowalski will immediately catch my bluff and kill me. Let me try writing it in SQL script form. He will not understand it, but I hope Neil will.

I logged into my Signal account and write the message in pseudocode. This looks like a SQL script, with all the syntax, but actually is not.

```
SELECT *thisisSos
uName = getRequestString("Sri");
uPlace = getRequestString("BtOnCam");
Ugps = getRequestString ("5211'23.73"N 005'31.67"E");
```

SQL = ‚GET * FROM Users WHERE Name =uName AND Place=uPlace AND GPS=uGPS'

It takes about ten minutes to do all these. Now I just have to keep my fingers crossed and wait for Neil to come. Hopefully he will get it. I have sent him everything, the place and the GPS coordinate. After all he is a detective in MI6, he should be able to crack this much.

Now I mainly have to pretend and play act. Pretend to hack the Secure Drop account. I know it is almost impossible, especially for an amateur like me. I still kept pushing in a few random SQL injection and phishing messages, and some random scripts from the command prompt in Kowalski's laptop.

The clock is ticking though. It is now almost forty minutes since Kowalski gave me his laptop. I am getting nervous now. Hasn't Neil seen the message yet? Or has he already been captured by these guys?

Sasha Kowalski's face is getting more serious. He takes the vial out of his pocket again. Sergei is standing blocking the door. What should I do? Should I ask for ten more minutes? Will he agree? Or is this really the end of my life?

Just as I look at Kowalski to ask for more time, I see a shadow behind him. My heart leaps, but this time with joy and hope.

A second later, the owner of the shadow kicks the door open and throws Sergei on the floor with a perfect karate uppercut. Looks like the giant passed out from being hit strategically on the Carotid Sinus.

Now I have the time to look at the intruder. It is Matt!

This sudden turn of events makes Kowalski briefly startled, and I grabbed that opportunity to snatch the vial from his hand and throw it on the floor. The deadly liquid spills on the floor. But it is not deadly unless someone swallows it, or it has direct contact with blood in any other way.

Sergei's gun is lying on the floor. In another twist of events, Kowalski grabs it and points it towards Matt. He has no other option than to raise both his arms up and stand in surrender. Sasha gestures me to stand beside Matt. I obey.

Sasha is now smiling. A click sound comes as he pulls the safety catch. Not sure who will go first… me or Matt…

Suddenly the glass on the window behind Kowalski is shattered. Startled, he looks behind and, just then, a pair of heavy boots enters through the broken window, kicking the gun out of his hand. Before he could pick it up again, the owner of those heavy boots also enters and knocks Sasha out with a massive punch. It is Neil, with a perfect, Bond-like entry.

## *The Mystery Unveiled*

"So, you must be the private detective employed by The Guardian, right?"

Neil asks Matt after handcuffing Sergei and Sasha. More police have come in by then.

"Yes," Matt replies with a smile.

"Then your agency is…" I start.

"… Matthew Holmes detective agency." Matt finishes the sentence.

"Good lord! Are you by chance related to Sherlock Holmes?" I ask.

"According to my grandma, yes. By I am not so sure, though." Matt smiles again.

"How did you come here, right at the climax?"

"I was on this case from the beginning, Sri. Reza messaged Mary Mason the day before he died. He told her that he suspects someone is watching over him and his life might be in danger. That's when The Guardian contacted me, to provide help to Reza. So, in a sense, Reza was my indirect client," Matt explains.

"Why you, Matt?"

"I worked with The Guardian before, in some other investigative journalism cases. Mary did not have Reza's full identity because he contacted her anonymously. But after his murder, she started suspecting that it was probably Reza. It got a boost when MI6 got involved in the investigation," Matt elaborates.

"That's why you were so keen on making me the baked salmon pasta for the dinner that night, Matt. You wanted information about Reza's murder from me!"

"That is so unfair, Sri! You were exhausted that day; I would have made you a dinner anyway," Matt protests. "But when I heard Reza was your professor and you are sort of a first-hand witness, I could not resist asking you a few questions," he admits, smiling.

"That's OK, Matt. I am not blaming you. Especially not after saving my life with your grand entry!" I smile back. Finally, I am feeling relieved.

"Right! Then I heard about the teapot incident from Sadia. After that you came to that Mayfair restaurant and started asking questions about those possible radiation poisoning. The next day Sadia told me about your scavenging through the college trash with Neil. So, it was getting clearer to me that you and Neil were fully into the investigation for Reza's murder." Matt explains further.

"So, you never really bought that Sri went to Scotland with me, did you?" Neil asks Matt with a smile.

"No, not really! But I thought MI6 wanted to keep it a secret. I would have never imagined in my wildest dreams that your boss is a double agent and you two are running from the internal enemies as well as the externals," Matt admits.

"Then how did you come here today?"

"Sri sent me a recorded video message this morning… a thank you message for her birthday wish," Matt smiles.

"But, Matt, I never said I was in Grantchester! I said I was calling from Edinburgh," I point out.

"Yeah, that's what you said in your recorded message, Sri. But the sign behind you, on the gate, read Nag's Head B&B, Grantchester!" Matt laughs.

Shit! How could I? Once again, I have proved that I am a sloppy sleuth, indeed.

"See! That's why I told you not to call anyone. It is easy to make mistakes like this," Neil points out, correctly.

"Well, ultimately it helped, didn't it? Matt came at the right moment," I remind him.

"That's true. So, Matt, what did you do after finding out Sri's location? Did you start immediately from London?"

"Yes. Yesterday, one of my informers told me about the problem between you and Daniel. So, I understood that you are being chased by ruthless foreign spies without getting much help from your department. Obviously, I did not suspect Daniel to be a mole, I just thought he was merely trying to avoid a complicated case and doesn't really trust you and your theories. But anyway, I started getting worried about the two of you. I thought I will come here and will talk to you, give you my real identity and then possibly we can work together and help each other. Never though I will enter at the very climax, though!" Matt explains.

"How did you know I was on the boat, Matt?"

"I did not! I went to the Nag's Head first, showed your picture at the reception and asked if could meet you. But they said you went out for a walk at the Little Meadow, by the twin weeping willows. Then I asked for the direction of Little Meadow. Still blissfully unaware that Kowalski has set a trap for you here."

"And your grand entry…?"

"Obviously I could not see anyone when I reached the weeping willows. I was just looking around. Then saw the boat and…"

"And you got suspicious with the flag there, right?" Neil asks Matt.

"Why? What's wrong with that flag?" I ask.

"Those three colours on the flag—red, yellow, and blue—they are the same as the old KGB or new FSB seal. Also, the symbol of the hawk, it is kind of their quasi-secret symbol; they use it for their internal communications. Not many people outside their internal circle know about it though!" Neil explains.

"How did you know about it then?" I ask.

"MI6 is not totally worthless either, Sri! If they can come and poison people with polonium on our own soil, then we can at least find out about their semi-secret internal symbols! Tell me Matt, what happened then? After you realized it could be an FSB boat?"

"Then I carefully approached the door, taking care not to be visible through any window. That part was not too difficult, though, because the blinds were closed on all the windows. I suppose because they did not want outsiders to see what they are doing to Sri inside."

"Right!" Neil nods.

"As I approached the door, I could see Sergei's head towering over the door frame and visible through the upper glass pane. Now this looked very suspicious. A gigantic figure like him guarding the door while all the blinds in the windows are closed shut. Given everything else that was going on, I did not want to take any risk, I barged in…"

"…With a perfect karate uppercut! And Neil, you?" I ask.

"I hopped on to my car and drove like crazy as soon as I got your message, Sri. I'll probably get fifty traffic tickets for all kinds of possible violations. But never mind that! As I was running towards the exact location, the boat on the Cam, as was specified in your cryptic message, I saw Matt barging in. He was probably two hundred meters ahead of me. Since he went through the door, I wanted to cover the other side. I didn't know how many were there, did I?"

"I see! So that's how Sherlock Holmes and James Bond together rescued the damsel in distress." I comment sarcastically.

"Nonsense! If there is any Sherlock Holmes in this whole saga, Sri, then that would be you. Sorry, Matt, no offence." Neil says.

"None taken." Matt is smiling, too.

"Sri is amazing. She cracked the puzzle of the murder weapon, with her alpha emitter theory. Excellent use of her physics knowledge, I must say. And she is the one who finally understood the identity of S and M."

Neil is all praise for me. I almost start feeling embarrassed. I am more used to him pulling my leg or shutting me down than him praising me like this.

"I know, Neil. She is very smart." Matt nods in agreement and then continues, "I should have thought about polonium myself, after all I have a Chemistry background. But got thrown by that low Geiger count. Was looking for something with a low half-life. The possibility of using an Alpha emitter never even occurred to me," he admits.

"Well, to be honest, that is more likely occur to a Physicist than to a Chemist. Radioactivity is a physics topic, is it not? Madame Curie was a physicist," Neil cheekily pulls Matt's leg.

"No, she was not! She was a Chemist!" Matt speaks like a true Chemist.

"Aright, alright! Since she got two Nobels, one and physics and one in chemistry, I guess both camps can put a claim on Madame Curie."

I cut them both off with my final verdict.

\*\*\*

The police take the criminals away with them. We are sitting in Nag's Head restaurant. The outside is a little chilly, so we are sitting inside, round a big, wooden table. It is not too crowded this time of the day, barring a few regulars. Mirella has also joined us. We will all head for London in a little while.

"All right, guys you have to explain a few things to me," says Mirella after putting her cup down on the table. "My background is in Linguistics. So please, what this alpha-beta-gamma stuff all about? How did you find out how Reza was killed?"

"OK… who can do it best? Matt?" Neil looks at Matt as he asks the question.

"Why me, Neil? Didn't you just say radioactivity is Physics stuff? You even hogged Madame Curie!" Matt winks.

"Come on, guys! Just because I don't have a science background doesn't mean I am stupid," Mirella sounds angry.

"If you explain it well, I am sure I can understand," she says.

"No Mirella, no one here thinks that you are stupid. The way you deciphered the message to figure out the Russian connection and got S&M's names, that surely deserves a lot of credit." Neil wants to calm her down.

"I am just thinking who can explain it best… Sri, why don't you give it a try? You are still in Uni, things are still fresh in your head."

I knew it was coming in my direction.

"Alright then, let me try."

I finish my latte and put the mug aside.

"Polonium-210 is a radioactive substance. You know what the main property of radioactive substance is, right Mirella?" I want to double check that I am starting from the right point.

"Well, I suppose they emit radiation."

Mirella gives the simple but right answer.

"Exactly. Now this radiation can be of three different kinds: alpha, beta and gamma. Out of these three, gamma is the electromagnetic radiation. Like the X-ray," I explain.

"And what about alpha and beta? Are they not like that, too?" Mirella asks.

"No. Alpha and beta both emit particles, like electrons, protons or neutrons. Beta particles are basically electrons, and hence extremely light but alpha particles are the heaviest among the three," I explain.

"OK, got it," Mirella nods.

"Alpha is actually a particle, a helium nucleus. Gamma, which has no particle, has zero mass; beta, which emits a single electron has negligible mass; but alpha which has two protons, and two neutrons has considerable mass."

"Got it. Then?"

"Now, most radioactive substance emit gamma rays. So, the Geiger Counter was invented by the famous Physicist Hans Geiger to detect gamma ray spikes."

"This Geiger Counter, does it measure gamma rays?"

"Well not directly. But gamma rays ionize the surrounding air—"

"Hang on a sec. What does ionization mean?" Mirella asks.

"Loosely speaking, gamma rays cause atoms in the air to become charged. A Geiger Counter measures that. More gamma rays mean more charged atoms in the air means higher counts in Geiger. Got it?"

"Yep." Mirella nods. "But what happens when alpha rays are emitted?" she asks again.

"That's the funny part. You see, as alpha particles are way heavier, they cannot move a great distance through the air. They just travel a few centimetres and then get dropped like a heavy ball. So, they cannot ionize the atoms in the air. Hence a Geiger Counter will never be able to detect the presence of alpha emission."

"I see! And since this polonium-210 emits alpha waves, the Geiger never caught them, right?" Mirella wants to confirm.

"That's right." I nod.

"But how did you get a slight increased reading inside the teapot then?" Mirella asks.

"Good question. Polonim-210 emits mostly alpha… let's say more than ninety percent. But it still emits some gamma radiation, less than ten percent."

"I see, those ten percent were detected in the teapot, right?" Mirella understands it right.

"Right. We were thinking the low reading is due to low half-life. It was not. It was due to the fact that polonium emits very little gamma," I explain.

"Why is this polonium so deadly? Like two billion times deadlier that cyanide or something, right?" Mirella asks her next question.

"Yes, Mirella, this is deadlier than cyanide."

"Why? Is it because Alpha is deadlier than Gamma?"

"Both are deadly. In different ways. Massless gamma can travel very far through the air. If we have a gamma emitter like radium, that will affect people even quite far away. That's why it is difficult to carry as a weapon for a very long time. The person who carries it will also get contaminated."

"How long will the effect of radiation remain?"

"That varies from element to element and depends on the half-life of the element."

"Half life?" Mirella furrows her brows.

"Means when the radiation gets halved. Let's say an element has a half-life of 100 days. That means after 100 days the radiation will be halved, after 200 days wit will be 1/4, after 300 days, 1/8$^{th}$ and so on and so forth," I explain.

"Wow! How long are these half-lives, typically?"

"It literally can be anything, Mirella. There are certain substances with half-lives of minutes or days. On the other side it could even be thousands of years for other elements. Now, if an element has a half-life of one day, then after seven days, virtually no radiation will be left. But if the half-life is hundred years, then it will continue to emit radiation and cause harm even after five-hundred years."

"Interesting! But why is alpha harmful? It cannot travel far through air, right?"

"No. That is why you can touch polonium-210 with your bare hands and nothing will happen. Your skin will act as a barrier, nothing will enter into your body. But if you drink it, then it will be deadly. Each of these alpha particles will then attack your individual body cells like bombs. It can destroy the crucial cells like bone marrow or brain cells or nerve cells. So, you will die in hours due to multi-organ failure."

"God! Is that what happened to Professor Reza Tavacol?"

"Yes Mirella, deadly poison. Once it enters the bloodstream, there is no cure."

"How dangerous. Lethal poison," Mirella exclaims.

"Not only that, Mirela, but this is also the perfect poison because it is so easy to carry and administer to the victim. The person carrying it will be totally safe. You will only a need a tiny amount, a vial full of solution is enough and all you need to do is sprinkle a few drops on the victim's food."

"Jesus! Thank God that polonim-210 is not readily available. Otherwise, murder would be so goddamn easy."

It seems Mirella now understands how the murder weapon worked. But Neil still looks a bit grumpy.

"What are you thinking Neil? How to gather evidence against Daniel?" I ask.

"Spot on, Sri. He cannot remain in MI6. But only my word, even if all three of you back me, will not be enough to remove him from his post. He can always say that he made a mistake, an honest mistake. We need hard evidence against him," Neil says.

"True. But you will get that, Neil. By tracing the footprint," I remind him.

"What footprint?" Mirella asks.

"I think Sri means the trail polonium-210 leaves. Isn't it, Sri?"

Matt smiles. He is right. After all, he has the right background.

"Spot on, Matt. Mirella, polonim-210 has an amazing property. It leaves trails. That vial, whoever has ever touched it, carried it or handled it … they will all have its mark on them. You will find traces of Polonium on Daniel's body, on his clothes, on his office furniture, car, everywhere. So, Neil, Daniel cannot escape. You will get your hard facts," I assure Neil. He looked much relieved now.

"But what happened to Helena? Why did Kowalski kill her?" Matt asks.

"She was just a collateral damage, Matt," I say bitterly.

"What do you mean?" all three of them ask together.

"Well, we have to run a few tests to be absolutely sure, but I have a theory how it happened."

"Do you? Spell it out then, Ms. Marple!" Neil comments.

"Reza's and Helena's labs have a common wall. On one side, there is the pantry in Reza's lab and on the other side there is spectroscopy dark room. The diffraction apparatus was set up, right by that wall, where I found Helena's body."

"So?"

Neil still can't follow my train of thought. Matt and Mirella also look like as if they are at a loss.

"I think this common wall has a leak. Perhaps the sealant there is gone. It is an old building, after all." I smile.

"Yes, it is a common problem in old buildings. My dad's house in Islington also had similar problem… there is a leak in the wall between the kitchen and the utility room. If water is spilled on the kitchen counter, the counter in the utility room also get wet—it's a nuisance, really. But what if there were a leak in that common wall between the labs, Sri? How is it connected to Helen's death?" Neil asked.

"I think Reza must have spilled the poisoned tea on the counter, while pouring it in a cup. Then that poisoned liquid seeped through the other side of the wall and soaked the diffraction grating papers, which were stacked against the wall."

"Jesus! And Helena got poisoned after touching those grating paper while setting up the experiment! Yes, that must be it, Sri, because polonium causes hair loss. That perhaps explains Helena's bald patches." Neil sounds excited. He has totally bought into my theory.

"But… how can Helena die just by touching the polonium-soaked paper? It's not that dangerous just to touch, it has to be ingested or inhaled to cause damage," Matt still sounds unconvinced.

"Not just by touching, Matt. Helena had a cut on her finger. I saw that in the morgue that day. So, when she touched the grating paper, polonium went directly to her bloodstream, causing her immediate death, within hours." I explain.

Neil, Matt, and Mirella all look stunned at my explanation. They remain silent for a while and then Matt speaks first,

"Wow, Sri, you are a true Ms. Marple. You solved a murder mystery by pure deduction and analytical skill. Neil, you just have to test those grating papers for the trace of polonium and that should be enough… What happened, why are you still frowning?"

"Yes, Neil, what's still bothering you?" Mirella also asks the same question.

"Sri, if that Sadia episode had not occurred that day, then you would have been in the spectroscopy lab, doing the experiments with those poisoned grating papers…"

Neil finally speaks to me in a dark voice.

"So, what Neil? Nothing would have happened. I don't have a cut on my finger like Helena, do I?" I want to lighten the atmosphere.

"This is serious, Sri. It could have been deadly. It does not have to be a big cut per se, you could have just scratched yourself with your nails, and that would have been fatal." Now Matt also looks very sombre.

"Nah, fat chance of that happening! I always clip my nails short, and unlike some people, I never scratch myself or others with my nails," I reply as I quickly glance at Neil.

## *Epilogue*

A month has passed since we returned from Grantchester. My life is back to normal again, revolving around my classes, labs, and friends. Classes are still a bit struggle though, as, including Kowalski, now we have lost three professors in total over the last one month. The good news is, a new member of faculty, Professor Wu, will join us from next month. Labs are also suffering from the staff shortage, especially the condensed matter lab, which lost both Reza and Kowalski in quick succession. Professor Yunis has stepped in, even though he has a theoretical background. But desperate times call for desperate measures, I suppose.

My status as an amateur sleuth has now been permanently established among my friends. However, that did nothing to dispel the myth of me being sloppy. The leg pulling and banter did not stop, but I think my friends are also proud of me, even though they try hard not to show it. Sadia has now moved to Hounslow Sisters to stay with her sister there and has got used to her new life and routine. Her relationship with Ed is also going at a normal pace, with no pressure from either side. I do not know what the future holds for them, but at least this a healthy atmosphere to let the relationship grow.

My relationship with both Matt and Neil, on the other hand, has now reached a new level. Matt is no longer just a flatmate, but he is now one of my closest and trustworthy friends. This has made our time together in our apartment really enjoyable. We talk, laugh, cook, and watch the telly together and I simply love his company.

The scintillation test done on the broken piece of teapot and the grating papers has vindicated our theories behind Reza's and Helena's death by polonium poisoning, and it has shot us to some instant fame. A picture of three of us came on the front pages of almost all the newspapers. It is indeed sensational news to find that a senior detective in MI6 worked as a double agent for the FSB, and as expected, this sensational revelation caused quite a ripple.

Daniel Morgan has now been suspended from his job and is being tried for treason and conspiracy. This polonium is a fascinating element; its full journey, from the moment it was put in the vial till the very end when it reached the victim's body can be traced by tracking the traces of alpha emission. As if it leaves an invisible ink trail all along its journey. So, there was really no escape either from Sasha or for Morgan, the infamous S&M.

Neil got significant credit for being persistent against all odds and finally exposing all these conspiracies successfully; he bagged a two-step promotion and is now working as a senior detective reporting directly to the anti-terror and investigation chief. So today he is giving me and Matt a treat at posh restaurant in Soho.

Even Aunt Shukla called me after seeing my picture in the news.

"Oh, my God, Sri, I cannot believe it… your face is on the front page! I am so proud of you, my dear. It's the blood, you see. My grandfather, your great grandfather from your mother's side, was known for his wisdom. People from all over the district used to come to him for advice. I told all my friends—Prachi, Sheila, Anu—everyone, that look, this is my family, so clever and wise. Now they would not dare bragging about those MITs and Oxfords. After all those institutes has thousands of students, but how many Sherlock Holmes do we have, eh?"

Aunt Shukla was happy and proud for me in her own way. But it is a different story with my parents. I even thought of not telling them about it, but it was too big a thing to suppress. Moreover, Aunt Shukla would have talked to them about it, anyway. So, I thought it would be better for them to know it directly from the horse's mouth.

"Sri! I thought you went to London to study, not to sleuth." said mum in a stern voice. "Who do you think you are? Sherlock Holmes?" she demanded to know.

"Why are you scolding her? She did a good thing, a brave thing, hasn't she? She was in the news, even your cousin Shukla is impressed. Yet you are scolding our girl…" I could hear baba's voice in the speaker phone.

"It's easy for Shukla to be impressed, she wouldn't have to worry about Sri's grades, would she?" Mum still sounded stern.

"You don't have to worry about her grades either, dear! Our Sri is sincere, she will take care of her grades herself, as she has always done. What if she wants to be a professional detective in the future?" Baba kept pleading for me.

"What? A detective? Why on earth? A nasty, rough, profession, always hobnobbing with the criminals… murderers and rapists… who in their right mind would like to do that?" Mum made her opinion quite clear.

"In fact, mum, a lot of people like to do it… Bakshi, Poirot, Holmes…"

"Stop talking nonsense, Sri. These are fictional characters. And they are all male. They can get into this rough business. Why would a decent lady take that as a profession? So very unladylike. You should pick up something respectable, like a job in academia or in the corporate world."

Mum gave her verdict. Now I understand why no fictional detective has got any parents. If they had, then their mothers would have made sure that the give up on chasing criminals and take some safe and 'respectable' profession instead.

It is completely different with Neil, though. His entire blended family is so proud of his achievements. Suparna of course firmly believes that Neil and I are dating, and no amount of denial is apparently going to change that. Neil once tried to tell her that I had to stay in his flat only to dodge the FSB assassins, but she paid no attention to that.

"That's OK Neil, we didn't ask for any explanation! Did we, dear?" She smiled as she looked at Aniket for support.

"No dear, we didn't." Aniket also smiled back without lifting his eyes from the book he was reading. Then he looked at me and said, "By the way, Sri, Linda wants to talk to you."

"Why?" I asked.

"Why not, Sri? Linda is Neil's mum. Why wouldn't she want to meet you? It's only normal," Suparna jumped in.

Both Neil and I understood it is futile to protest, let them think whatever pleases them. But the good thing is, Suparna has also managed to hack a few messages exchanged between Morgan and Sasha. It made the case against them even stronger. Neil didn't say anything, but I think he was feeling bad for his suspicion on Suparna that day.

"This evil stepmother stereotype is very deep rooted, Sri. Children get indoctrinated to it from a very early age. Just look at our fairytales, from Hansel and Gretel to Cinderella, this stereotype is bolstered everywhere." Neil told me.

But I do not blame him much. When his own boss, a senior detective in the state intelligent agency turns out to be a traitor, working as a double agent for an enemy country, then it is normal to lose faith in everyone.

As I am waiting for Neil and Matt to join me at the restaurant, I think of Aunt Shukla's words. After heaping the praise on me for cracking this case and making it to the front page, she went back to her usual nosy self.

"Sri, who are these two men with you in the picture? One of them is your flatmate, Matt, I suppose. He is very handsome, I must say. But who is the other one?" she asked after looking at our photo in the newspaper.

"Neil Basu, detective, MI6." I answered in a matter-of-fact way.

"Neil Basu… seems like I heard the name somewhere… is this by any chance Suparna's stepson?"

"Yes."

"Oh, I see! Anyway, be careful. Don't get into any hanky-panky business with him. Theirs is a weird family, all these blended family nonsense with divorced partners and stepchildren. They are not like us." She gave her snap judgement. Mum and she have this one thing in common; they both are very prone to pass snap verdicts. Perhaps it runs in the family.

My train of thought is interrupted as both Neil and Matt enter the restaurant together. We take our seats, order our drinks, and start chatting.

"To Neil, the senior detective, MI6." Matt raises his glass.

"Cheers!" I also join in.

"Thanks! So, Matt, your detective agency is now kind of famous, I can see. When are you giving us a treat?" Neil asks, smiling.

"Any day! Yes, the agency is now a lot busier. Looks like I have to recruit more staff." Matt also looks happy.

"That's good! In fact, if you want, I can recommend a few. I have some connections." Neil wants to help.

"That would be wonderful. Thanks, Neil."

"Nothing to thank me for, Matt. We often need help from such private detective agencies. We keep a kind of list, the ones which are good and trustworthy. I will put your agency's name in there."

"That will be really great, Neil, thanks! We also need help from the police, too, you see. Symbiosis." Matt smiles as he sips his drink.

I am witnessing their incredible bromance in silence.

"But to be honest, I already have my eyes on someone. If she agrees, then I will hire her at the drop of a hat," Matt's smile widens.

"That would be a good choice, no doubt. But will she agree?" Neil winks.

"Hmm, I don't think she will agree, either. It would have been good though, if she did, but I think she will prioritize her studies first."

"Besides, Matt, do you really want a sloppy sleuth in your agency?"

"What? Were you talking about me?" I finally realize.

"Look Matt! It took so long for her to get it. Didn't I tell you? The sloppy sleuth!"

"I—I didn't understand. Because I was not expecting anything like this." I admit.

"That's the problem with you, Sri! You never really realize that some people may want you!" Neil feigns a sigh.

"Couldn't agree more," Matt agrees.

"But on a serious note, Sri, if you want to become a professional detective, then I suggest you learn a few things." Matt comments.

"Such as…?" I enquire.

"Like judo or karate or some other martial art. Neil or I will not always be there to save you." Matt comments bluntly.

"No way! I can't do those things. They hit people hard and throw them on the floor. So tough, I will die!" I summarily dismiss his suggestion.

"Then, perhaps, a gun?" Neil suggests.

"Not sure I can do that either. You see, I have astigmatism, cylindrical power in my eyes. I can't even pop the balloons at the country fair with those toy guns," I admit frankly.

"I see! So, no weapon. Can you drive? Ride a bike? Swim at least?" Neil keeps asking.

"I can ride a bike, very slowly though, but don't know how to swim. I can drive, though."

"At least a saving grace. Where did you learn to drive? Here?"

"No, in India."

"I see. Then it can be used as a weapon as well, you can kill people with your chaotic driving, I am sure!"

They give a high five to each other and start laughing heartily.

"No need to be so dismissive, guys, I am not a professional detective like you." I feel a bit annoyed.

"True, but you know what I think? Even if we cannot employ one another officially, we can still work as a team," Neil suggests.

"For sure. The trio of Neil-Srija-Matt. Other detectives, beware! You have competition." Matt says dramatically.

"Well, you two are pro. But what about me? I am a student, I have my studies," I say.

"That doesn't matter. You will come running if we get an interesting case. I am sure about that." Neil sounds confident. Then he smiles and says, "But I am a bit worried that I may be a bit left out; after all you two live in the same flat, you can discuss things all the time. I will be the third wheel."

"That's bollocks, Neil. During this case you two were staying together, as a couple! Maybe you two should date," Matt winks.

"Or maybe you two." It's Neil's turn now.

I thought this is high time that I put a stop to this passing the ball game, once and for all. "Listen, if we have to work together as a team, then we need to set some ground rules." I jump in with my suggestions.

"What ground rules?" They both sound doubtful.

"Like we, in the trio, will never date one another. We will keep things platonic between us."

I give my wise suggestion which unfortunately is met with a lot of scepticism from my two friends.

"That's crazy, Sri! What rule? It's all about consent, if any two mutually agree then that's it," Matt dismisses me summarily.

"Which two would mutually agree?" I ask.

"Any two; you and me, you and Neil, or Neil and me."

They both wink and started laughing mischievously.

"You guys are impossible. Suit yourselves, but I will keep the ground rules for myself. We are a good team, and I don't want to mess it up by adding emotional angle to it," I declare firmly.

"You know what I think, Neil? Sri is afraid that she will not be able to resist us unless she imposes those hard rules on herself." Matt winks.

"Spot, on Matt. She wants to save herself for her future husband."

I know that Neil made the obnoxious comment on purpose, to pull my strings.

"Blimey. Is that what it is, Sri? Are you saving yourself for your future husband? Where did you come from? The 18th. Century?" Matt asks in disbelief.

"No, that's absolutely bonkers! Loads of crap from Neil. I am not saving myself for anybody. But I do have a few criteria for my future partner, and I am very particular about them." I tell the truth.

"Do you? What criteria? I'm curious, what could they be? Which none of these two very eligible bachelors can satisfy?" Matt asks with a mischievous smile.

"May I hazard a guess? She probably wants an Indian." Neil makes another outrageous suggestion.

"Wow! That is racist. But Neil, you are half Indian, will that do? And for me, let me see… well, I can always use Google Translate." Matt winks.

"Again, loads of crap. My future partner could be from any goddamn background, Chinese, African, Indian, European, literally anyone." I protest.

"Well, what's wrong with us then? Why won't you date either of us?"

"Nothing! But we are a good team, and I don't want to ruin it with romance."

"Why would romance ruin it?" Neil asks.

"I have the same question." Matt seconds him.

"It will. Romance will ruin it for sure. I don't know about you, but I will keep the ground rules, from my side." Now it is time for me to pass my snap verdict. It runs in the family, after all!

"What a shame! I think we are missing an opportunity here," says Matt as he sipped his drink.

"Well, I am not," says Neil, as he got up from his chair and went straight towards the blonde sitting at the bar. She had been checking him out for quite some time now, I noticed. In a few minutes, Matt also gets up from his chair and waves towards a girl at the table on the other side of the room. I turn around and see Gina. Matt says, "Excuse me," and goes ahead to join her.

Men!

Well, screw them all.

I order another Margarita.

# Reviews of Alpha Beta Gamma

"Witty and intellectual, *Alpha Beta Gamma* introduces a highly charismatic amateur sleuth who risks everything to unravel a sinister international political conspiracy." – BestThrillers.com

" Ray has created an appealing lead sleuth to navigate this complex and winding case, which offers plenty of surprises for readers. With clever characters and sharp storytelling, this is a stimulating, timely, and creative tale."
--Self-Publishing Review

"Malabika Ray's Alpha Beta Gamma is a really great mix blend of mystery and suspense, led by what is almost a unicorn in contemporary trade literature: an Asian female protagonist." --Readers Favourite.

## About The Author

Malabika Ray was born and raised in India, and she migrated to Europe for her work in 2005. Since then, she has lived and worked in Nice, Paris and London and Stockholm.

Malabika has a masters in Applied Physics and heads and engineering division at a Swedish car company.

Alpha Beta Gamma is her first novel where she utilized her professional knowledge with her interest in global politics and weave an intriguing spy thriller.

Malabika lives in the suburbs of Stockholm with her husband, daughter and Merlin, the cat.

Interested readers can contact her at,
malabika.ray.author@gmail.com

Malabika Ray

# The Sloppy Sleuth and the Trio Series

At the end of Alpha Beta Gamms, the self-proclaimed sloppy sleuth, Sri, teams up with MI6 agent Neil Basu and the Private Investigator Matthew Holmes.

In the subsequent novels in this series, this Trio will embark on many other adventures, solving historical mysteries taking on foreign spies and unearthing hidden treasures across the Europe. As they do so, they also navigate through the complexities of their own relationships and lives in general.

There will at least be five more books in this series and possibly more.

Alpha Beta Gamma

Malabika Ray

Printed in Dunstable, United Kingdom